MASCOTS

FRANCIS OWEN DREWREY

AVENTURIER PUBLISHING

Published by Aventurier Publishing

www.aventurierpublishing.com

DEDICATION

To my wonderful wife, for 24 years of patience.

ACKNOWLEDGEMENTS

As a first time author, I have benefitted from the invaluable advice, thoughtfulness, and effort of several talented industry professionals. Andrew Pate has generously shared his decades of experience with me so that I could move the book from a draft to a final product. Mark Kohut agreed to edit and proofread *Mascots*, but added considerable value by providing excellent suggestions for clarifying and strengthening the story. Kristy Buchanan, of KN Design, designed a cover that creatively captures the essence of *Mascots* as well as the attractive and readable interior. They have all made the entire process fun and edifying and I appreciate their kindness and patience with a rookie.

Michael Gaines and Jeremie Denley, who put themselves at risk on a daily basis, provided useful information and insights on the practices and procedures of municipal fire and police departments.

I was fortunate to have three good friends – Ivan Stahn, Windy Sawcyzn, and Casimir Pulaski – read an early draft of *Mascots* and offer many useful suggestions for improving the clarity of the story and enhancing the characters.

Finally, I would like to thank my wife and children for their unwavering support and encouragement during my on again, off again work on *Mascots*.

I

The sun would not rise for another two hours, but the important work of building the future could not wait for daybreak. The team setting up the camp had been working for only 30 minutes, but Michael was very pleased with the progress he saw. His team had been planning this for several weeks. All the equipment and supplies they would need to get started had been purchased and brought to the site. Everyone was working hard and everything appeared to be on schedule. Even the weather was cooperating, an auspicious sign. Michael had checked the weather forecast two days ago and it had warned of a sixty percent chance of rain this early Monday morning. But now, looking at the weather app on his iPhone, Michael saw a series of full sun icons for the first hours of the day. When the new day dawned on Freedom Plaza, the people of Morgan Springs and of the University would get their first glimpse of the Occupy Morgan Springs encampment under a clear, blue mid-October sky.

Morgan Springs, with a population approaching 50,000, was on the small side for a franchise of the Occupy Wall Street movement. However, because the town had a large and nationally recognized university, Morgan Springs enjoyed an urbane sophistication that rivaled that of much larger cities. Located in the South, there were countless joints serving great fried chicken and barbeque. Yet, the town also boasted chefs and restaurants which had won James Beard awards and had solidified the town's national ranking as a "foodie" paradise. Residents generously supported the University's repertory theatre and concert series and were rewarded with world class performances. A town with cosmopolitan tastes, Morgan Springs boasted the highest per capita readership of the *New York Times* of any community in the United States outside the New York City metropolitan area.

In addition to being an intellectual and cultural oasis in the southeastern United States, the town enjoyed an enviable level of economic security. Morgan Springs was a modern company town of sorts with the "company" being a large public university and its affiliated hospital. These institutions ensured a predictable flow of taxpayer, student, and patient dollars that rose steadily almost every year. The town was also within commuting distance of the state capital and many state employees chose to live in Morgan Springs. This reliable influx of money from the federal and state governments, and a continuously growing student population, insulated Morgan Springs from the recessions, layoffs, and other economic setbacks faced by people who might live just a few miles beyond its borders.

With its nationally recognized university and its energetic and progressive citizens, this small city was a fount of social change in what was once Confederate territory. It boasted the first African-American mayor in a Southern town with a white majority. Also, the town claimed bragging rights for electing the state's first openly gay mayor. It sat in the only county in the state to give George McGovern more votes than it gave to Richard Nixon in the 1972 Presidential election. Evidence of the town's progressive credentials ranged from the names of its heroes placed on parks and streets to the pithy slogans appearing on the bumper stickers that decorated vintage Volvos and sleek new hybrids.

One of the few conspicuous reminders of a less enlightened past (and an irritant for some) was the statue of a Confederate soldier, saber drawn, facing north on perpetual guard for the next Yankee incursion. He had been placed there in 1895 by a Confederate veterans' organization. For most, he was just another part of the downtown landscape. But every so often, a small group would make a stink about this symbol of a more benighted era and demand the statue's removal. They were usually countered by five or six members of the local chapter of the Sons of the Confederacy (some of whom looked so old they may have been, in fact, the actual sons of actual Confederate soldiers). Whether a source of pride or embarrassment, the ever vigilant soldier proved to be a failure at protecting Morgan Springs from the dreaded Yankee invaders. In recent decades, more and more people were coming to Morgan Springs from north of the Mason-Dixon Line for the University, the jobs, and the quality of life. Two of the three most recent town mayors were born in the Northeast: one in Pennsylvania and one in Brooklyn. And, as if to underscore the poor Confederate's impotence, fraternity pranksters would steal his sword every few years forcing the Sons of the Confederacy to solicit donations from members to buy replacements.

The town's Freedom Plaza was the civic heart of the town making it the obvious place for Occupy Morgan Springs to take root. Throughout the year, citizens and groups set up tables here to spread diverse viewpoints, organizations would recruit or hold fundraisers, and sports fans of the University's teams would celebrate here after victories. Most local civil rights activities or protests in the past two decades had started here. In addition to being a center for civic activity and celebrations, it was also a focal point for the expression of shock and grief. Candlelight vigils and memorials were held here for the sudden, unexpected death of a University student. It had also served as a natural place to assemble and grieve after the September 11, 2001 attacks on New York City and Washington.

Michael thought about how he and his team of occupiers had chosen this place for its symbolic value as well as its location. They believed that what they were doing fit with the pattern of the many previous protest activities that had begun here. Michael saw himself as the newest general in a social justice army that had been fighting a long war against oppression. In his opinion, this central square, long associated with activism by members of the community, would be the best place to launch and run the next long battle in the never ending struggle.

His reflections were interrupted by the sound of an approaching car. Since traffic on Washington Street, the town's main street that passed Freedom Plaza, was almost nonexistent at this hour, Michael had no trouble identifying the old Toyota Corolla. The car had a unique sound as well as being one of the ugliest cars in town. Its collection of bumper stickers, some new and some badly faded, clearly advertised the political sentiments of Josh Wilbanks, Michael's friend and mentor. Josh had come to check on the progress of the occupiers in Freedom Plaza.

Josh was able to get a parking space just across the street from the Plaza. The streetlights gave him a good view of the activity underway and he was impressed with what he saw. It looked like about two dozen people were in the Freedom Plaza erecting tents, putting up tarps for shelters, setting up tables, and hanging banners. One large tent was being loaded with supplies in anticipation for the long campaign ahead.

As Josh got out of his car, he saw Michael and another young man, who looked barely old enough to be in college, walking toward him.

"So, what do you think?" Michael asked, with a faint smile that telegraphed pride in what he and the other occupiers were about to spring on the town.

"Everything looks great," Josh responded. "This has really come together. People are really going to be blown away when they see this."

Michael introduced the young occupier who accompanied him, Daniel Russo, and Josh to each other.

"So, are your ready for battle?" Josh asked Daniel.

"You bet," Daniel answered, looking toward Michael for approval. Michael nodded in agreement. Daniel continued, "We can barely wait for sunrise to get here. Everyone is really cranked up. But, I have to admit, I'm kinda nervous. I wonder what the town and the police will do. The cops are a bunch of fascists and they might beat the hell out of us."

Both Josh and Michael knew that Daniel and the other occupiers were unlikely to get their heads bashed in with night sticks or tear gassed or tasered or suffer any other harm at the hands of the Morgan Springs Police Department. This was a college town and neither the town police nor the University security ever did much about a little creative politics. Michael recalled an incident when he was an undergraduate at the University. Some students, who ran one of the campus' parody magazines, created an issue that mocked a campus performance of *The Vagina Monologues*. The budding satirists published the first installment of "The Chronicles of Commander Cocky," a cartoon which followed the adventures of a six-foot, anthropomorphic penis. A feminist group on campus was incensed and retaliated by collecting all of the copies of the magazine they could find and publicly burning them. Two of the arsonists were seen and reported to campus security.

The women had to appear before a college dean, who explained to them that a university was a place for diverse opinions and, unfortunately, this included parodies that offended feminists. But, aside from this mild rebuke, the women suffered no consequences for their theft and arson. The dean reserved the majority of his anger for the sophomore humorists. He basically told them it was their own fault that twelve hundred copies of their publication were destroyed. As he explained, they had written something offensive and they should have expected this sort of reaction. Furthermore, the young men should have realized that their satire might make women on campus feel vulnerable, threatened, and perhaps traumatized. The lads were incredulous that adult women would feel endangered by a cartoon phallus but, at this point, they had gotten the message about how things really worked at the University. They knew better than to waste the dean's time arguing about trivialities like the First Amendment, or to whom it applied. The first installment of Commander Cocky's campus adventures would also be the last.

The bottom line was that the Morgan Springs Police Department and the University security tended to look the other way in such cases of more "spirited" political expression such as the theft and burning of reading material. There were never any serious repercussions. Of course, Josh and Michael were not going to disabuse Daniel of his unwarranted concerns about getting his head beaten in. They could remember what it was like when they were freshly minted idealists like Daniel and how the potential for some friction with law enforcement added to the excitement of civil disobedience. They would not rob Daniel of the special thrill of sensing imminent danger or his romanticized notions of fighting for a noble cause at great personal risk. Michael and Josh thought the worst case scenario was that the occupiers would be ignored as just another part of the college town scenery. There was certainly nothing heroic or exciting about that.

"Yeah Daniel, I know what you mean. They really are a bunch of bastards," Josh responded with a tone of sincere concern. "I really admire you. You're all taking a huge risk and really putting yourselves out there. I hope nobody ends up in the hospital."

While Josh and Michael were not concerned that the local police "fascists" would beat on Daniel and the other members of Occupy Morgan Springs, they were concerned about the level of support the movement might get from the community.

They would soon learn that they had nothing to worry about.

• • •

Two hours later, the first thing in the camp that the sun's rays illuminated was the largest of several banners. It proclaimed "Occupy Morgan Springs: We Are the 99%" in dark blue lettering on a white background. The banner hovered about 20 feet above the concrete of the Plaza and was the only thing in direct sunlight for several minutes. Its stark white background gave it a brilliance in the early morning sun that boldly announced that things were going to be very different in Morgan Springs.

After several hours of hard work preparing the Plaza, the occupiers were ready to take a break and admire their camp under the first light of the new day. A pot of coffee was percolating on a propane camp stove and someone brought in several boxes of donuts. Michael emerged from his tent after donning his uniform of the day. He was wearing military style boots with camouflage pants and a black North Face fleece jacket to ward off the early morning chill. Once it got warmer, he would peel off the jacket to reveal a white tee shirt with an encircled letter "A," the symbol for anarchy. His ensemble was topped off with a black beret which made him look even taller than his six foot, three inches.

As the sun climbed in the sky, the tents began to fall under its light and their colors could be fully appreciated. There were blue ones, green ones, and several REI brand tents with their distinctive colors. Most appeared to be two-person tents and were arranged in a tight and orderly manner. There was one open area of about two hundred square feet, but this would be filled tonight by some homeless men who Michael had recruited and provided with tents he purchased at an army surplus store. The men had expressed interest in hanging around with Occupy Morgan Springs and the plan was for them to "spontaneously" join the movement to convey a sense of growth and dynamism. Their addition would leave the Plaza completely filled with tents by the second night giving Occupy Morgan Springs the appearance of being on the verge of bursting out of Freedom Plaza.

The occupation's command post was under a 12 by 12 foot tarp on poles that provided shelter from the sun and rain. A similar tarp would be used as a food prep area. A large family tent, dubbed the "Taj Mahal," was used for storage. This larger tent would have been a more comfortable place to sleep and would allow campers to stand up, but having occupiers sleeping in the "Taj Mahal" would run counter to the movement's egalitarian message.

The Occupiers also set up the "People's Library" in one corner of the Plaza. The library was a folding utility table covered with dozens of low quality photocopies of pamphlets, many self-published. The pamphlets included the thinking of gay rights groups, feminists, radical environmentalists, ethnic separatists, anarchists, socialists, communists, and groups known only to themselves. They included the trials and tribulations of political prisoners and ideological martyrs including the famous such as Mumia Abu-Jamal as well as many who were unknown. How-to pamphlets covered everything from "herbal abortions" to making your own organic, vegan cat food.

The reading material was free, but there was a large glass jar for donations. It contained between two and three dollars of loose change. The jar was also seeded with one crumpled $5 bill, put there in the hope that it would spur greater generosity from any donors.

The Occupiers had already been up for hours, but with a round of hot coffee and sugary donuts, they were re-energized and ready to engage the people of Morgan Springs and the University. They were excited about the change they would bring and could not wait to share their vision of a better world with a receptive public.

II

Rev. James Dawson (known around Morgan Springs as Reverend Jimmy) pulled into the St. Paul's Church parking lot and eased his Toyota Prius into his spot designated for the Senior Pastor. He had passed Freedom Plaza on his way to work and had taken note of the crop of tents that had sprouted since he left the church Sunday afternoon. The church office opened at 8:30, but he was 20 minutes early, so he had time to grab a cup of coffee at the Starbucks on Washington Street and see what was going on at the camp. He had been following the news of the Occupy Wall Street movement in New York City and elsewhere and wanted to check out what the local crowd had cooked up.

Jimmy was now in his eighth year as St. Paul's senior pastor. He had once hoped to move up in the church hierarchy, but that was unlikely, at least in the region around Morgan Springs. While he was generally in step with the national church leadership on both spiritual and secular matters, Jimmy and his congregation were seen as more politically liberal than the denomination's other churches in the state. It was unlikely that the pastors of the other churches would support him if he tried to pursue a regional leadership position. And, it was even less likely that the lay leaders of those other churches would support him. Despite having his ambitions of climbing the church hierarchy frustrated, Jimmy had carved out a comfortable life for himself and his family in Morgan Springs. As the senior pastor of a large, university town church, he had a fairly decent salary and benefits package. He was able to supplement his income with adjunct teaching gigs at the University as well as royalties from a book he wrote on religion and politics that appeared on the syllabi of many college courses.

During his time at St. Paul's, Reverend Jimmy had built a solid reputation as one of Morgan Springs' political movers and shakers. Dawson prided himself on being at the forefront of local social justice activities and engaged in a bit of friendly competition with the other progressive clergy in the community. He kept an informal tally of how many letters to the editor he and his rivals had published in the local papers. He also took pride in the fact that he had been arrested for civil disobedience seven times. While this was no record for Morgan Springs – that belonged to a retired pastor from the African Methodist Episcopal Church who compiled an insurmountable record during the 1960s – Reverend Jimmy led among active members of the clergy. In his mind, it was only natural that he would be the first of his peers to get on board with something like Occupy Morgan Springs.

After leaving Starbucks with his coffee in hand, Jimmy walked to Freedom Plaza and surveyed the camp from the sidewalk. He wondered if he might know some of the occupiers, but he did not immediately see anyone he recognized. However, several of them seemed to know who he was and greeted him with warm smiles.

"Hey, Reverend Dawson," called a young woman as she walked over toward him. She was not a churchgoer, but knew of Dawson's activism and was pleased that this local progressive icon was showing interest in their camp. "I'm Katie Olin. Thanks for stopping by," she said as she extended her hand.

"Glad to," he replied, taking her hand, "and, please, call me 'Jimmy.' This was quite a sight when I drove into town this morning. I was hoping we would get something like this here in Morgan Springs and, well, here it is, right in the center of town."

"You should join us. You could help us throw some Wall Street moneychangers out of the temple," she suggested.

Jimmy laughed at the biblical allusion. "I certainly like the sound of that. Perhaps I will."

"Can you christen our camp? Maybe, you know, sprinkle some holy water on it?" she prodded humorously.

He laughed again. "You might have to go over to St. Francis and find a priest for that. My church doesn't use holy water, but I am with you in spirit, and you and all your friends will be in my prayers."

Jimmy scanned the camp and could sense the excitement and energy of the young occupiers. He looked at a group of three men who appeared to be discussing or planning something. One of the three was Michael. With his trim, athletic build and the addition of the beret, he looked significantly taller than the other two men and this gave him a commanding presence. For Jimmy, Michael's body language, beret, and height imbued the young man with charisma. Reverend Jimmy assumed he must be the leader of the occupiers.

"Well, I'd better get back to the office, Katie. Good luck with what you are doing here. I'm glad that young people like you care enough to do this."

"Thanks for stopping by," she replied.

Jimmy took a sip from his coffee and began to walk back to St. Paul's. He thought what these young people were doing was important and he wanted to see this movement succeed in Morgan Springs. He began to wonder if Jesus were to come to Morgan Springs with his disciples in the 21st century, would they set up shop in Freedom Plaza to spread their revolutionary message like these occupiers?

"What Would Jesus Occupy?" he thought, chuckling to himself. What would be the right way to respond to a backpacker tent-dwelling Jesus and his band of energetic, idealist camper-disciples? He decided how he might be able to help the occupiers. At the corner, he turned around, and walked back toward Katie.

"Katie, I may be able to help you and your friends in a small way. It looks like you're planning on staying here awhile. I can't imagine what your sanitation situation here is, but the people camping here are welcome to use our facilities. There are bathrooms obviously, but we also have a shower, if that would help."

"Thanks. That would be awesome," she responded. Her appreciation was genuine since the Occupy Morgan Springs planners had not thought through the bathroom issue fully. They had planned to spread this need out, so to speak, among a range of downtown businesses and public restrooms. However, they did not know how long businesses would tolerate the use of their facilities by non patrons.

"I can't get you 24/7 access because we have to lock up the building at some point every night," Jimmy added. "But I will get back to you later today with the hours that would work. In the meantime, here's my telephone number. Don't hesitate to call if there is anything I can do to help. "

He gave Katie his cell phone number and then left again for St. Paul's.

Technically, it wasn't Jimmy's call to make an offer of the church's facilities like that unilaterally. As senior pastor, he was responsible for the spiritual side of things at St. Paul's. An elected lay committee was responsible for the church's finances and property. There was no telling how long the occupiers would be around and it would be for the lay leaders to sign off on something like this. Of course, Jimmy proposed things all the time and approval from the lay leaders was mostly a formality, but they were still supposed to be included in decision making. But in this case, Jimmy just strongly felt that supporting the occupiers was the right thing to do. It would be easier to ask the lay committee for forgiveness later than to ask for permission now.

After dropping off her son at his high school, Linda Burr needed to run several errands and drove to downtown Morgan Springs to get money from the ATM at her bank. Parking in the downtown area was usually a challenge, so she was pleasantly surprised to find a parking space on a side street just off of Washington Street and only a short walk from the bank. Better yet, the driver who recently vacated the space had left 17 minutes on the parking meter so she would not have to fish around in her purse for change. She could easily get cash and return in that amount of time.

After exiting her car and reaching the corner of Washington Street, she looked up the street toward her bank and could see that something was going on in Freedom Plaza. As she walked up Washington Street, she passed by Freedom Plaza and the bustling occupation encampment piqued her curiosity. She decided that she would have to stop for a minute or two on her way back and see what was going on.

Linda returned a few minutes later and took in the whole scene – the banners, the tents, lots of young people, the buzz of activity. The excitement was contagious. A sign designating an area as the "People's Library" caught her attention and she walked over to the table. There she found stacks of photocopied materials addressing a range of causes and viewpoints. Many of the titles seemed to be about obscure issues and causes so she picked through several of the pamphlets without really reading them. By doing this, she could take in what was going on around her in the Freedom Plaza without looking like a gawker.

"See anything good?" asked a young male occupier.

"Very interesting stuff," Linda answered, trying to sound noncommittal to hide the fact that she wasn't exactly sure what she had just been reading.

"I'm Pete. I'm sort of the Camp Librarian, I guess. What do you think of all this?" he asked looking around the Plaza with obvious pride.

"Impressive," she responded, still trying not to be pinned down on anything. "So how long is this going to go on?"

"As long as necessary," he responded boldly. "We know that change isn't easy and we are prepared to stay here until we make it happen."

"So what are you planning to change?"

"Well, to be brief, the world, but mostly the dominance of Wall Street and our failed capitalist economy in this country." Sensing her attentiveness, he continued. "Most of the wealth and power in this country is controlled by a small minority of people and they have pretty much stolen democracy from the rest of us. It's time for those of us in the 99 Percent to rise up and take it back."

Pete paused briefly and continued, "Since you have not walked away yet, I assume you are not part of the One Percent."

"Uh, no, of course not," Linda responded, with a look of mock horror.

Linda had read about the Occupy Wall Street movement in New York City and was intrigued that something similar, although on a smaller scale, had taken root in Morgan Springs. She took an interest in this young man, probably about the same age as her son in college. Pete had not shaved in a while, but it did not look like a full beard was in his immediate future. He had mild, but not repellant, body odor and she thought he smelled faintly of marijuana. Despite that, Linda found him intriguing in a bad boy, rebel sort of way. She could imagine that young women his own age might be attracted to him.

Linda listened to him talk about the need for dramatic change in American society, the movement's plans, and their vision of the better world they sought to create. His excitement about being part of rapid and momentous change was infectious and resonated with Linda. She found herself nodding in agreement as he spoke.

Linda began to think about how this movement mirrored what she remembered from the late 60s and early 70s when she was a young girl. Linda was not even 10 years old when Woodstock took place. But she had vivid memories of the era – the music, the clothing, the anti-Vietnam war protests. As a young child, she had been too young to fully appreciate the politics of the day, but she had sensed the air of rapid change and unlimited possibility. Big and exciting things were happening, and it was people not much older than Linda who were making those things happen.

During those years when Linda was growing up, her main conduit to the sixties zeitgeist was her older cousin, Karen. She recalled spending two weeks one summer with this cousin when Linda's family and her aunt's family vacationed together at the beach. Linda had been about ten years old that summer. Karen was nineteen.

Karen provided a window into the exciting life that Linda could expect when she got older and went away to college. Karen wore the clothing of the era that Linda could only envy because her mother would not let her wear "hippy" clothing. Karen hung out with kids her age on the beach at night, smoking cigarettes and drinking wine. Karen exposed Linda to music that was a lot wilder than the Three Dog Night songs she heard on Top 40 radio stations. Karen had a boyfriend who played bass in a campus rock band. Better yet, during the summer vacation, Linda overheard her mother and her Aunt Elaine discussing, to her pre-teen mind, the ultimate transgression. Karen was having sex with the boyfriend.

From Linda's perspective, Karen's world was completely independent from the boring and colorless world that Linda felt she inhabited. She assumed that Karen was playing a role in the protests and other forms of youthful rebellion she saw on television. Karen was the model of the new, independent woman that Linda hoped to become someday. From the perspective of an elementary school student, college life and its freedoms held the promise of a glorious time of uninhibited exploration.

Soon enough, she was old enough to attend college herself. But, Linda did not find the highly energized and exciting campus life that she had imagined earlier. The music she had listened to with Karen was still around, but she was more likely to hear New Wave music at parties. Those wearing tie dye shirts and sporting long fuzzy hair had to share the campus with a new breed of students who dressed out of *The Official Preppy Handbook*. The whiff of cannabis was common, but its use seemed to be more of a private than communal thing. The air of rebellion had given way to a new era of conservatism ushered in by the election of Ronald Reagan.

Like many of her college peers, Linda adopted the spirit of the times and set aside any illusions of radically changing the world. She tried marijuana a few times and lost her virginity during the second semester of her freshman year but, otherwise, her college years were relatively tame. She chose to major in Communications, finished her degree in four years, took a series of several jobs in PR firms, got married, and had two sons.

And then, quickly, painlessly, she was fifty years old.

Seeing the youthful Freedom Plaza occupiers, their commitment, and their energy had collapsed the last 40 years of Linda's life. It took her back to the time when she first yearned to be part of something like this. Of course, she realized that she was too old to hang around with this crowd. She was certainly not going to trade her four bedroom home on an acre lot for a tent in the middle of Freedom Plaza. But, these young dreamers excited her. She admired their zeal and their idealism. Her heart was with them.

Linda pulled out a ten dollar bill and added it to the "People's Library" tip jar. She only realized that she had spent a half hour listening to Pete when she got back to her car and found a parking ticket under the windshield wiper. Her free parking space would now cost twenty-five dollars. However, the visit to Freedom Plaza was like being given a second chance at the dreams of her youth. It left her feeling too lighthearted and rejuvenated to care.

IV

Frederick Hutchinson, Editor of the *Morgan Springs News*, received a text message from Jennifer Harper. She let him know that a group had occupied Freedom Plaza in the style of Occupy Wall Street and that she would be interested in getting to work on a story immediately.

Hutchinson, who went by Fred, had just hired Jennifer the previous spring after she received her B.A. in Journalism from the University. He had been pleased to get her to come to the *News*, especially given the paper's limited budget. Jennifer was a promising young journalist who seemed to have a knack for being in the right place at the right time. During her time as a student journalist, she had attended innumerable Town Council meetings and had learned how to navigate the egos and eccentricities of the town's politicos. As far as this new development in Freedom Plaza went, it made perfectly good sense for Jennifer to handle it. As a recent University graduate, this would appeal to her idealism. Fred guessed (correctly) that she was already getting burned out covering Board of Education and Town Council meetings. He also thought, being young, Jennifer might be able to develop some rapport with the occupiers and might even know some of the people involved. He quickly returned her text message with his consent to prepare an article for the next edition.

Hutchinson was a former Associate Professor from the University's School of Journalism and had been serving as the Editor of the *Morgan Springs News* for several years after his retirement from academia. The *News* was published three times a week – Wednesday, Friday, and Sunday. Although it sold for one dollar, almost all of the *News'* revenue came from advertising, especially automobile and real estate advertising. A majority of town residents never actually paid for it since they could find it in their driveways for free. Although anything of news value could be gleaned from it in three or four minutes, many Morgan Spring residents still looked forward to the *News* because it supplemented their daily news sources with good information on local high school sports and the details of Town Council and other local meetings. It also included the colorful observations and thoughts of local columnists and citizens who sent letters to the editor.

The best part of Fred's job was that he got to use the editorial page as a platform for expressing his opinions on the issues of the day. Fred had always admired the journalists and editors of the Jim Crow era South who had bravely and unapologetically taken a lead in the battle for civil rights. He had not started his own career in journalism until after the Civil Rights Act and Voting Rights Act were passed so he could only imagine the role he might have played had he been practicing his craft during the 1950s and early 1960s. To some extent, he felt cheated. It was as if he had been put on the earth to participate in a war that would alter the course of history, but a cruel delay in the timing of his birth caused him to miss the key battles and he could join the fight only as the war was winding down.

Missing out on the height of the civil rights era meant that the warrior journalist had to find his battles where he could. As the saying goes, the pen is mightier than the sword, and Fred wanted to wield the pen as often as possible. True to his deep interest in the civil rights era, his interest in an issue was greatest when the issue had a racial angle. An example was when Morgan Springs debated changing the name of one of its main thoroughfares to Martin Luther King Jr. Boulevard. Hutchinson was naturally for it and wrote an editorial supporting the change. For the most part, the community also supported the idea. At the time, over 700 communities in the United States had already named a roadway after Dr. King and it seemed natural that Morgan Springs would maintain its progressive bona fides by joining this club. However, Hutchinson was troubled to learn that a small group, largely composed of business owners with businesses on the road, did not want the name change. The principal reason the business owners cited was the trouble and expense of changing the addresses that they had been using for years on letterhead, business cards, websites, and signage.

For Hutchinson, providing editorial support of the name change to honor the civil rights leader was not enough. He believed it was also critical to impugn the motivations of the business owners who felt they would be burdened by the change. Fred acknowledged that it was possible that some of the business owners might genuinely be concerned about the cost and trouble of the name change. But, he reasoned, the best that could be said of them was that their opposition to the name change was rooted in their selfishness and lack of community spirit. Fred was certain that the most plausible reason for rejecting the change was the ingrained racism of the business owners. He wanted to make sure that all the readers of the *Morgan Springs News* were aware of the darkness in the souls of these dissenters. Although the name change was broadly supported in the community, Fred felt it was necessary to write four editorials. Each one was more merciless toward the business owners than the previous one. When the Town Council unanimously voted to approve the name change, Fred was delighted with this fresh evidence of Morgan Springs' progressivism. But, what delighted him most was the imagined despair of the businessmen who had opposed the change.

Fred had been following the coverage of the Occupy Wall Street movement in New York City and was thrilled at the prospect of having this sort of activity in Morgan Spring so that the *News* could cover it. It was a local story, he was sympathetic to the cause, and it seemed like an excellent opportunity to promote the things he believed in. He knew he wanted to write an editorial supporting the occupiers and he had a pretty good idea of what he would say. However, he felt it best to venture over to Freedom Plaza and actually see the occupation camp for himself before writing something. He put on his navy blazer, pulled at his paisley bow tie to straighten it, and headed out the door for the walk in the crisp, autumn air.

V

Mayor Steven Worthington was not particularly surprised to learn that occupation activity had begun in Morgan Springs. Although the Mayor perceived himself to be a fairly standard Morgan Springs progressive, he was on friendly terms with the local crowd who played at the fringes of the political spectrum. He had assumed that something like this was in the works. The Occupy Wall Street activity in New York City, Oakland, Seattle and other American cities was national news and he liked the idea that his small Southern town would be joining this club.

Worthington had been mayor for almost three years and his election as mayor was largely a matter of luck, or more accurately, the bad judgment of his predecessor Richard Winston. Mayor Winston, hoping to increase tourism in the Morgan Springs area, had pushed the Town Council members to authorize a marketing research study to assess the town's image as a tourist destination. The town solicited four bids for the research project and Winston sat on the committee that assessed them. He then leaned on his fellow committee members to choose the most expensive of the four bids. After the contract for the study was awarded, an executive from one of the losing firms cried "foul" and complained that the winning marketing research firm was owned by the sister of Mayor Winston's partner. While this might or might not have meant anything by itself, it was also revealed that the winning firm's bid was about 40 percent higher than the other three bids. Furthermore, there was no compelling evidence that the winning firm's proposal was any better than the losing firms' proposals.

The scandal metastasized fairly quickly. The aldermen who had followed Mayor Winston's lead and voted to hire the firm felt misled and exploited. The *Morgan Springs News* estimated that the inflated bid would put tens of thousands of dollars directly into the pocket of the sister of Mayor Winston's partner. In most years, town residents might have looked the other way. But, Morgan Springs had just increased its property taxes and there was also discussion about possibly increasing sales taxes. It was not a good time to be giving away the taxpayers' money to friends of the Mayor. It became apparent that Winston could actually lose his bid for re-election.

Steven was approached by two aldermen and asked to run for mayor. He was indeed interested in political office and had thought he might want to run for the State Senate or even the U.S. Congress some day. Now was as good a time as any to launch a political career. The aldermen who recruited Steven thought that Winston, with some serious opposition and a scandal hanging over his head, would step down after one term to avoid a bruising primary that he had a high likelihood of losing.

Instead, Winston decided to dig in and run for re-election. His supporters quickly went on the offensive and attacked the Worthington campaign for its "hate-fueled bigotry." They described the complaints over the overpriced marketing research study as a "phony scandal" and declared that the real issue was that "the Mayor loved another man." However, as Mayor Winston had been elected after sailing through both the primary and the general elections as an openly gay man – and had even appeared at many campaign events with his partner – it seemed disingenuous to complain that progressive Morgan Springs had suffered a sudden outbreak of homophobia.

The next line of attack was to go after Worthington's wealth. It was common to condemn wealth in Morgan Springs because, as one of the most affluent college towns in America, there was so much of it to condemn. The town had some of the most expensive homes in the state and its streets were full of European and Japanese luxury cars. Many of the town's leaders lived in those homes and drove those cars. Yet, anyone could play the (lack of) wealth card and attack the shameful cupidity of others. Under the right circumstances, even the merely affluent or financially comfortable could be likened to the infamous robber barons of the Gilded Age by their political opponents.

Indeed, Worthington had been born to an affluent local family. After getting his undergraduate degree in Political Science at the University, he attended law school at the University of Virginia. While his background, education, and profession left him well positioned to enjoy the good life, he opted to provide legal services to undocumented immigrants. His wife's salary as a corporate counsel, and a bit of family money, allowed the Worthingtons to live in a 4,300 square foot house in one of Morgan Springs' most expensive neighborhoods and to send their two children to an exclusive, private school. But, by doing the work of the angels, Steven was able to maintain that he had repudiated the privileges he had enjoyed from birth. The Winston campaign's noise about Worthington's wealth would be largely ignored.

After a bitter campaign, Worthington won the Democratic primary with 54 percent of the vote and went on to win the November general election with 81 percent of the vote against token Republican opposition. Despite the solid win, Steven always wondered if it was a bit of a Pyrrhic victory. His predecessor had not been remarkable or unique in his ideas, policies, or leadership style. He was a standard Morgan Springs progressive. But, Winston was valuable to many in Morgan Springs who felt he gave the town a certain cachet. He made many residents feel like the town was "a few degrees cooler" than other communities since they could boast that their town had elected the state's first openly gay mayor. Steven Worthington had taken that away from them and there was some lingering resentment at what was perceived to be his opportunism.

The Mayor was now coming to the end of the third year in his four-year term. Although the next general election for town offices was a little more than a year away, Steven had to think about the upcoming primary in May. He was pretty sure that one of the town's aldermen, Tom McFadden, would enter the primary and he would be in the middle of a heated campaign in just a few months. McFadden had been a loyal ally of Mayor Winston and would be able to count on the support of many former, embittered Winston supporters. Of course, if Worthington could get by McFadden, the general election in November would be a mere formality.

In order to stay ahead of the likely challenger McFadden, and possibly even scare him off, the Mayor needed to think about how to utilize Occupy Morgan Springs. It was perfectly clear that the occupiers were violating the town's regulations for Freedom Plaza. There was a rule against spending the night in the Plaza and the occupiers indicated that they intended to break that rule indefinitely. Some of the community would certainly object to the occupation and would expect the town to enforce the regulations and make the occupiers leave. At the same time, it was already clear that the occupation was generating interest and excitement among many who took pride in having their very own occupation in Morgan Springs.

The Mayor had to think through the political implications. Even though anyone who was a serious player in local politics took pride in describing himself or herself as a progressive Democrat – with the exception of a few ancient radicals who unapologetically identified themselves as Socialists – Worthington had to navigate the subtle, but critical, distinctions among political groups. A new resident of Morgan Springs or an outsider might see a fairly homogeneous political class. But, those new to the local political scene would not be politically astute enough to know who was truly on the cutting edge and who was behind the times.

For example, almost all of Morgan Springs' political heavyweights had Obama-Biden 2008 bumper stickers on their cars and would proudly display them until their cars disintegrated into piles of rust. Obama-Biden yard signs had remained in some yards for months after the 2008 election, not due to oversight, but to serve as an ongoing reminder of the homeowner's superior virtue in having been part of the election of the first African-American president. However, despite the near unanimity of support for Barack Obama among the town's leaders, there was still a caste system of sorts among the local politicos. Those who had supported Obama early in the 2008 Democratic primary process held a higher place in the political hierarchy than those who had initially supported Hillary Clinton. The few people whose first choice had been John Edwards in the 2008 primaries were at the bottom of this hierarchy. The "Two Americas" rhetoric that Edwards used during his 2008 campaign had been attractive – and was, in fact, echoed in the slogans of the Occupy Morgan Springs campers – but ultimately, he was unsuitable. The problem was not that he had a child with a mistress while his wife was dying from cancer, or that he suffered the humiliation of being fodder for the National Enquirer, but that he was neither a woman nor a minority. Perhaps if Edwards had been bisexual or Latino, his supporters might have been able to hold their heads higher.

Like the Mayor, many people in town were supportive of the global Occupy Wall Street movement and what was going on in Freedom Plaza. They also liked to think of Morgan Springs as being on the leading edge of social change. This activity at Freedom Plaza was new evidence of the town's status as a beacon lighting an otherwise benighted corner of the nation. They were not going to cede their hard-earned and rightful place as the vanguard of Southern progressivism to Athens, Georgia or Chapel Hill, North Carolina or another city. The occupation and the occupiers were going to be a source of civic pride for the people of Morgan Springs. The Mayor decided it would be political suicide to take that away from them.

He would direct the Town Manager, Bill Wingate, to ignore the regulations on the use of the Freedom Plaza. Wingate, in turn, would instruct the Morgan Springs Police Department to not enforce the regulations.

Occupation Morgan Springs now had the Mayor behind it.

VI

Burke Thornton came into downtown Morgan Springs to meet his friend, J. T. Shelton, for lunch at their favorite burger joint, the Corner Cafe. The Corner Cafe never got the memo about the dietary dangers of salt, cholesterol, and saturated fats. They specialized in half-pound burgers topped with several types of cheese or bacon or chili or combinations of the above. The most popular side was a large order of seasoned fries served in a paper towel lined bread basket to soak up some of their grease. This fare was most popular with University students who were too young and thin to care yet and working class townies like Burke who had been eating here for years.

If anyone asked Burke what he did for a living, he simply told people he was a plumber. To some extent, this was true. He had started out that way as a young man, but now, in his fifties, he could better be described as the owner of a large plumbing company. He had 27 people working for him and a fleet of 11 trucks. It did not hurt his feelings that he was the guy you called to unclog your toilet because he earned more than most of the faculty members and administrators at the University. And while some of the faculty might have tenure, he had even more job security. Issues with your plumbing did not get put off for another day, and the work was not going to be outsourced to another country. Unlike some other Morgan Springs residents, Burke did not try to give the impression that he was tormented by his affluence. He had joined the ranks of the affluent only after decades of hard work and obsessive dedication to his customers. He enjoyed his success without apology.

Burke had taken a few detours on his road to relative prosperity. As a teenager, he had been a good student in high school and was able to realize his childhood dream, admission to the University in Morgan Springs. Money was tight for the Thorntons, but Burke's parents were excited for him to have this opportunity. There was one advantage to being one of the poor kids on the idyllic University campus. He could not afford the distractions – alcohol, spur of the moment trips to the coast, the fraternity scene – that would have prevented him from excelling at his studies. His passion became the exploration of Western history and thought from the time of the ancient Greeks. During his freshman year, he decided that he wanted to double major in history and philosophy. He even dared to dream of attending graduate school.

Due to his family's financial situation, Burke started each semester wondering if it would be his last. Ultimately, the fall semester of his junior year proved to be the end of his college career when his father died unexpectedly just before Thanksgiving. It would have been possible for the Thorntons to scrape together loans and other funds to keep Burke in college, but a more pressing issue was that his mother and younger siblings needed the income that he, now twenty years old, could provide. He completed the semester and left campus at the Christmas break to begin his adulthood sooner than expected.

Burke's hard work in supporting his family and later building his plumbing business did not leave him with much time for hobbies. However, he never lost his enthusiasm for history and philosophy and, with money being scarce at times, the price of a library card was always right. Because he never received the piece of paper that declared him to be an educated man, he continued to educate himself. In his twenties, he had envied the students who stayed the whole four years, attended the graduation ceremony in their brilliant red caps and gowns, and received their diplomas. Later, he came to realize that maybe he was the fortunate one because his education never ended. For too many in his cohort, the diploma was the culmination of a box checking exercise that demonstrated worthiness to future employers, potential spouses, and social peers. But for Burke, serious inquiry and reflection about life's big questions would be an ongoing process. College had only been a start.

As Burke got older and began to experience life as an employed adult, a husband and father, and an involved citizen, he began to apply his self-education to current events and contemporary politics. He liked to write letters to the editor of area newspapers, comment on blogs that addressed both local and national events, and engage in spirited debate on the issues of the day. It was an understatement to say that his views did not fit with the dominant ethos of Morgan Springs. However, while Morgan Springs' minority of conservatives and libertarians suffered in silence, Burke was not the least bit reticent about expressing his views. He strongly believed that the First Amendment was a terrible thing to waste.

Burke arrived at the restaurant to find J. T. already seated in one of the window booths. He ordered a jalapeno-cheddar burger, while his friend opted for a mushroom and Swiss burger. The two men's concession to healthful eating was to order only one large basket of fries and split it. They spent most of the meal catching up on what each man's adult children were doing as well as the woeful performance of the University's football team during the previous Saturday.

As they picked at the remaining fries, it was getting later into the afternoon and the lunch crowd began to thin out. With things being less hurried in the restaurant, Nancy, their waitress, became chattier when she dropped by to refill their iced tea glasses.

"What do you think about what's going on in Freedom Plaza?" she asked.

"There's something going on?" Burke asked. "Is there a protest?"

"It looks like kids from the University have turned it into a camp." Nancy continued, "The Plaza is pretty much filled up with tents. There is a banner hanging over the Plaza that says 'Occupy Morgan Springs'."

"Oh, good Lord," moaned J. T. while shaking his head. "Don't they have classes to attend or papers to write?"

"So it looks like Occupy Wall Street has come to Morgan Springs," Burke said with a wry smile. "I've gotta go over there and see this."

J. T. tended to see eye to eye with Burke on most things political, but lacked his zeal for engaging those from other parts of the political spectrum. "I need to get back to work," J. T. responded. "You're on your own, Burke. Say 'hello' to the hippies for me."

The friends paid their checks and left the Corner Cafe with Burke heading in the direction of Freedom Plaza.

On his way, Burke passed the sad, brick shell of Tabor's Variety Store which had been closed for at least a decade now. He thought wistfully about the role the store had played in the community when he was a child. It had been part of the rhythm of life in Morgan Springs – the place you went to load up on school supplies in the fall, to buy a last minute Mother's Day present, and, of course, to do your Christmas shopping. Its place in the community had been strengthened by the fact that it was owned by a local family, the Tabors, whose five kids had each put in his or her time working in the store. But, the parents were now deceased and all five of the children were now grown and had moved away. The Tabors, once central to the community, deserved a better tribute than this empty eyesore.

After walking five blocks, Burke arrived at Freedom Plaza to find the occupation in full swing. The novelty of the campsite plus the gentle warmth of the October afternoon had brought out dozens of students and townspeople to see what was going on. Some people were chatting with occupiers, some were reading the slogans on the various signs and banners, and others were perusing the offerings of the People's Library. He wandered over to the library table to check out the literature.

Although the reading material covered a range of topics, Burke quickly noticed that some of the materials were especially edgy, even shocking. The occupiers were offering full reprints of the entire Unabomber Manifesto, the work of the infamous serial bomber Ted Kaczynski, who sent exploding packages to scientists and others involved in work he found objectionable. He had been dubbed the Unabomber because his victims included employees of universities. Burke thought it was unusual that, in a university town, the occupiers were getting inspiration from someone whose bombs killed three people and maimed and injured almost two dozen educators and scientists. Burke also found a pamphlet entitled "Sabotage on the Job for Fun and (Loss of Your Employer's) Profit" to be interesting. The pamphlet provided dozens of vignettes detailing the ways in which unhappy employees could wreak havoc in their workplaces and undermine their employers. Techniques included everything from making deliberate errors when filling orders for customers to actual destruction of delicate and expensive machinery. He found this odd in light of the fact that many of the occupiers' signs demanded a solution to the nation's high level of unemployment. Yet another pamphlet, from a radical environmentalist organization called the Gaia Action Front, described arson attacks on residential developments in the Pacific Northwest. While this radical group did not claim responsibility, it clearly approved of and celebrated the millions of dollars of destruction wrought in order to save the planet.

Burke looked up from the table and noticed a sharply dressed man with a familiar sartorial touch. He did not know Fred Hutchinson personally, but recognized him from his picture, with an ever present bow tie, that appeared with his columns in the *News*. Burke could tell that Hutchinson was looking at one of the

Unabomber Manifesto reprints. The stunned look on Fred's face was unmistakable.

"They've certainly provided some interesting reading material," Burke said in Hutchinson's direction.

"This is unbelievable," Hutchinson responded with a wide eyed look and slight shake of his head. "Just unbelievable."

VII

On Wednesday morning, the third day of the occupation, Burke Thornton walked out into his driveway to pick up his daily newspaper as well as his free *Morgan Springs News*. The occupation activity at Freedom Plaza was the main topic of conversation in town and he wanted to see how it was presented in the *News*.

The front page's headline read "Morgan Springs Occupied" and the headline's large font added a breathlessness to the announcement that put the occupation activity on a level with the end of World War II or the 9/11 terrorist attacks. The three-quarter inch high headline appeared over a large color photograph that captured the entire, tent-filled Freedom Plaza under the "Occupy Morgan Springs: We Are the 99%" banner. The byline read, Jennifer Harper. The article quoted some of the occupiers and discussed their goals as well as how the local activity was related to the Occupy Wall Street activity in New York City and elsewhere. It also provided detailed information about the number of tents and campers in Freedom Plaza, inside information on how the occupy site would operate, and background information on Michael and Katie, the leaders of OMS.

The article continued inside the paper and included a photograph of Michael that Jennifer had taken. Because of the *News'* limited budget, Jennifer often had to take the pictures for her articles. She did not consider herself to be a talented photographer, but she was especially pleased with one of her shots of Michael. The photo she used caught the charismatic Michael gazing into the future from under his beret. The expression on his face conveyed both pain and defiance. The black and white image made him look iconic and, in Jennifer's assessment, pretty hot.

Burke moved on to Fred Hutchinson's domain, the editorial page and, as expected, he found the lead editorial addressing the occupation at Freedom Plaza. Burke recalled that the literature offerings from the People's Library had made an impression on Hutchinson, and unsurprisingly, the editorial mentioned the reprints of the Unabomber Manifesto as well as the Gaia Action Front's pamphlet celebrating the arson attacks on homes. But, as Thornton read, he was astonished to learn that Hutchinson's take on these materials differed completely from his. For Hutchinson, the literature celebrating murders, bombings, and destruction was not evidence of a movement which might have violent inclinations. Rather, the inclusion of such material merely revealed the "inchoate ideology of a burgeoning movement" as if the choice of taking a peaceful or violent approach to social change was not much weightier than choosing where to go for lunch. Furthermore, Hutchinson was impressed by the occupiers' promise to stay in Freedom Plaza as long as necessary. From his perspective, this intensity and militant tone was all the evidence he needed that their world view was correct and their cause was just.

The Fourth Estate, like Town Hall, was fully behind the occupiers.

• • •

As the first weekend of the occupation approached, Occupy Morgan Springs was on a roll. The Mayor had instructed the Town Manager and the Morgan Springs Police Department to hold off on enforcing the Plaza regulations. The occupiers had a green light to stay at Freedom Plaza for the near term. As a bonus, they were allowed to use the Plaza's outdoor electrical outlets to power their computers and other appliances as well as charge their smart phones.

Another church had followed Reverend Jimmy's lead and offered additional restrooms. One downtown restaurant offered occupiers a ten percent discount. Another restaurant, not to be outdone, competed vigorously for the occupiers' business with a twenty percent discount. The board of the local grocery co-op, the Healthy Planet Market, voted to allocate some of its members' dividends to OMS and also to supply them with bulk foods at cost.

The *Morgan Springs News*, with Jennifer Harper on the beat, would continue to provide sympathetic coverage. The occupiers had been speaking with reporters from other area newspapers and expected more favorable coverage over the weekend and into the next week. A local alternative weekly paper, *Aux Barricades*, had one of its people spending nights in Freedom Plaza so the *AuxBar*, as it was nicknamed, had an embedded reporter.

The occupation was developing a large fan base in other quarters as well. Residents would show up every evening at six o'clock to watch or participate in the nightly occupier meetings. Although the fall semester was well under way at the University, three professors from the sociology department altered their course plans to incorporate the Freedom Plaza activity. Similarly, a professor of Political Science teaching a course called "American Revolutions: Protest and Political Action" gave seventy of his students an excuse to hang out in Freedom Plaza for credit. Several social science teachers in the public middle and high schools gave their students extra credit for visiting the camp and occupier meetings.

Jennifer, with her journalist's instincts, could not help noticing that many of the young female visitors to Freedom Plaza gravitated to Michael. Without exactly understanding why, she resented the way this growing band of groupies seemed to look for excuses to hang around him, to flirt with him, and to laugh lustily at anything he said that was even mildly funny. He seemed to be nonchalant about the attention and did not appear to flirt with his admirers, which only enhanced his mystique and desirability.

In addition to being big news in town, attention to Occupy Morgan Springs had begun to extend beyond the town and county. Katie updated the OMS website on a daily basis so the outside world could follow the Freedom Plaza activities. Occupy Morgan Springs was linked to hundreds of blogs and websites that tied it to the larger Occupy movement. She also established an Occupy Morgan Springs Facebook fan page and watched the number of people indicating that they "liked" OMS climb by the hour.

The plaza's several thousand square feet were now filled with tents. As Michael had planned, more tents housing homeless men appeared the second night. The sight of a packed tent city gave the impression that Occupy Morgan Springs was on the verge of spilling beyond Freedom Plaza into the streets.

Support for OMS was not unanimous. Some websites and blogs run by conservatives in the state did not want the Occupy Morgan Springs activity to go unanswered. One ridiculed OMS as hillbilly wannabes running a lightweight version of the Occupy Wall Street camp in New York City. Another included a picture of the Freedom Plaza camp with a heading that read "Mayberry Occupied!!!" A conservative student newspaper at the University proposed a fundraiser to buy soap, deodorant, and lice treatment for the occupiers. But, for the most part, OMS' detractors remained quiet rather than compete with the deluge of reflexive praise.

Despite the warm reception and the general sense that the occupation was something in which Morgan Springs could take pride, tears were beginning to appear in the town's civic fabric.

The Occupation displaced various community groups which had requested permits to use the Plaza for blocks of time on weekends. This space was a well located venue and was a favorite of teams, church groups, and scouting groups for their fundraising. One of the first casualties was a girl's soccer team that sold holiday wreaths and garlands every fall. Because the occupation now took up the entire Plaza, there was no place for the team to set up their display and take orders. The girl's soccer team was the first group of many to learn that, despite signing up for time slots weeks in advance, they were out of luck. Calls to Town Manager Bill Wingate's office never reached Wingate himself, but only a sympathetic receptionist who could only say that the situation in Freedom Plaza was "complicated" and "things were being sorted out" and that she would pass along complaints to the Town Manager.

Also, despite its putative seriousness and world-changing mission, OMS had engendered a party atmosphere in Freedom Plaza complete with open consumption of alcohol and marijuana. Apparently, the new society the occupiers were working for would not have any hang-ups about the public use of intoxicating and mind altering substances. The public drinking and drug use violated the Freedom Plaza regulations but, as the prohibitions on overnight stays and structures were not being enforced, it seemed logical to assume that other rules could be similarly ignored. The occupiers were quick to take advantage of and revel in this absence of limits.

Soon, the generosity of some local restaurants and churches had emboldened some of the occupiers with a sense of entitlement. Many were disrespectful to merchants and would argue that they should be given discounts, or even free merchandise and food, because of the nobility of their cause. It was assumed that any restroom in a Washington Street business was for broad public use and some business owners resented this presumption. One business owner was enraged when a pair of occupiers decided that his restroom, with its lockable door, would provide more privacy for afternoon sex than their tent in Freedom Plaza. When he decided to limit use of his restrooms to customers, he became a target for verbal abuse.

• • •

Having won the hearts and minds of (most of) Morgan Springs, Michael and his lieutenants assessed their situation. They had successfully occupied the Plaza without any pushback, but this movement needed to be more than an urban campout. Michael had gotten involved in Occupy Morgan Springs to fight a corrupt system. It was time for a meaningful challenge to the One Percent. All of his lieutenants agreed.

It was time for Phase II.

VIII

The manager of the downtown AmeriBank branch unlocked one of the bank's front doors to open it for business. After checking the area outside the front doors, he was disgusted to see a clump of excrement right where one would have to stand to use the ATM machine. If there was any doubt as to the source of the pile, that was put to rest by the sight of several soiled paper napkins with Starbucks logos which had been used for toilet paper. One clean paper napkin had a message scrawled on it – "Here's my 'night deposit,' assholes." Given the rhetoric he had been hearing at Freedom Plaza for the past week, the manager could only assume the culprit was one of the occupiers.

While beginning the disgusting, but necessary, task of cleaning up the mess, the manager surmised that his day could not get any worse. He was wrong. The overnight deposit had only been a warning of things to come.

Two blocks away, at Freedom Plaza, a group of 75 occupiers was assembling for Phase II and the event of the day: Occupy AmeriBank. The plan was to disrupt the bank's activities and prevent it from doing any business. Some of the occupiers had initially suggested filling up the lobby with so many bodies that bank customers could not get in. However, Katie and others were concerned that this would be going too far since they would be on bank property. However, they came up with an alternative tactic that would meet the same objective. After a brief discussion of logistics, they voted unanimously on their next move.

The group left the Freedom Plaza in a single file line chanting "AmeriBank steals / for the One Percent." Most of the group members were dressed in dark, mostly black, clothing and many wore hats making them hard to distinguish from each other. As they filed down the sidewalk, they encountered several early morning passersby. However, OMS had been in Freedom Plaza for about a week, so the sight of the occupiers was no longer surprising or noteworthy. They had become part of the downtown landscape.

Once the occupiers arrived in front of AmeriBank, they donned masks or bandanas to cover their faces. They also tightened their line. The marchers then formed a continuous, closed loop that was long enough to block all the doors to the bank's building. With the loop in place and the occupiers marching tightly behind each other, hands on shoulders, anyone who needed to enter the building would have to push through two noisy lines of quickly moving bodies. The occupier loop was now a writhing, menacing snake biting its own tail.

The bank manager, already furious about the malodorous night deposit, came outside and stood in the building alcove, now sealed off by the revolving occupier snake.

"You're blocking the entrance to the building. You need to move on," he yelled, wondering if he could even be heard over the chanting.

"This is a public sidewalk, asshole," an occupier shouted over the din of the revolving mob.

"We have First Amendment rights, too. Just because you're a bank and have all the money doesn't mean you're the only one who gets free speech," yelled another.

The bank manager wondered if there was any point in calling the MSPD. Could the occupiers even be forced to leave? They had been allowed to camp in Freedom Plaza, they were being protected by Town Hall, they got puff pieces in the *Morgan Springs News*, and they pretty much seemed to have the run of the town. At this point, he had no confidence that any laws would be upheld or that businesses like his bank would be protected.

The occupiers' plan to disrupt the flow of customers into the bank was working. During the day, there were usually at least three or four customers in the bank lobby at any one time and sometimes more. However, no customer was willing to push through the continuously moving double line of masked marchers. Every so often, a customer would ask to be let through, but the occupiers ignored the request and kept up the march. None of the bank's customers, showing up alone, wanted to directly confront the marchers.

The first break in the occupier snake occurred about 20 minutes after the beginning of the march. An attorney, with an office in the bank building, was running late for an important conference call. He observed the marching occupiers for less than a minute. His anger mounted as he thought about how ludicrous it was to be kept out of his own office by a protest. He had seen enough and decided to act.

He moved toward the line. The occupiers nearest to the attorney saw him approaching with a determined look. They each grasped the shoulders of the marchers in front of them more tightly to strengthen the barrier. The attorney saw what they were doing and moved to slide between what he judged to be two of the scrawnier occupiers. He then proceeded to pry his way through both lines simultaneously pushing his frame through the bodies and pulling arms off of shoulders. He did not know if the masked occupiers would become violent, but he was ready, in fact eager, to start swinging if necessary. However, the occupiers had been instructed to refrain from physically attacking anyone. Occupy Morgan Springs was, after all, a non-violent movement. Of course, it could not be helped if people were intimidated by their actions and covered faces.

With their continuous loop broken by the attorney, and with a sense that it might be time to stop taxing the patience of bank patrons and employees, the action leader decided it was time to leave. He gave a command for the protesters to disperse and the snake broke into pieces. In order to commemorate the occupiers' victory over AmeriBank, one masked occupier pulled a can of red spray paint from under his jacket and sprayed "OMS" on the ATM machine and then sprayed each letter on three different glass doors at the entrance of the bank building.

The vandalism of the bank was supplemented by the shooting out of several store windows along Washington Street. Several occupiers had concealed air pistols under their clothing and could surreptitiously and quietly shoot windows as they walked by. It created a powerful and disconcerting effect for onlookers who wondered if the windows were shattering spontaneously. The casualties included the window of a drug store, the window of a tee shirt shop, and the passenger side window of a Mercedes-Benz (presumed to be owned by a member of the One Percent). Masked and clothed similarly, the occupiers were able to commit the vandalism anonymously and without fear of surveillance cameras. With this anonymity, the vandals could simply remove their masks and bandanas and blend back into the town scenery.

IX

After the march on the bank, Katie and Michael realized that the smashed windows and spray paint on Washington Street would have a negative impact on public perceptions of OMS. They wanted to make sure that their interpretation of the post-march vandalism was disseminated.

The afternoon after the march on the bank, while getting a cup of coffee at a Washington Street coffee shop, Katie saw Jennifer Harper sitting at a table working on her laptop.

"May I join you for a minute?" Katie asked. "There's something I need to discuss with you."

"Sure, Katie. What's up?"

"I know you'll be writing a story about our protest at the bank this morning."

"Actually, I'm working on it now."

"Oh." Katie paused briefly before getting to the point. "You know, Jennifer, we don't know for a fact that the vandalism that occurred after the protest was someone from OMS. We hope it isn't portrayed that way in the *News*."

"So, if it wasn't OMS, who was it?"

"We can't be certain. It might have been one of ours, or it could be someone trying to make us look bad. We certainly did not authorize it. We fully take ownership of the peaceful protest in front of the bank. But, Michael and I don't think it would be fair for the movement to get blamed for the vandalism if it was not something we authorized."

Jennifer felt uncomfortable. She admired Katie but there was also something about Katie that bothered her. She was not sure if she wanted to help. But, as she thought more, she realized the real source of her ambivalence about Katie was jealousy. Katie and Michael were a strong team who worked well together. While they had different talents and roles, they seemed to be of one mind – like a couple who had been married for decades. Jennifer figured that Michael resisted the attention of his groupies because he was involved with Katie. It all made sense, but she had to probe.

"You and Michael seem to have thought up your PR on this one. You two make a good team."

"He's a very talented guy. I enjoy working with him."

"So, are you two . . . ?" Jennifer trailed off before finishing the question but Katie did not need for her to finish it.

"Oh, no," Katie answered with a smile. She sensed that Jennifer was not simply making casual conversation. "If you're interested, he's fair game, as far as I know."

Jennifer decided it would be no problem to help Katie.

• • •

About an hour later, Jennifer stopped by Freedom Plaza. Michael spied her and walked over.

"Hi, Jennifer. Katie and I have been looking for you. We wanted to talk with you about this morning's march on the bank."

"Katie and I talked. I saw her about an hour ago getting coffee at Java Man."

"So, can you help us out?"

"Of course, Michael." She paused and added, "Anything you need." She made sure her eyes locked to his as she said the last three words. After a few seconds, she saw a faint smile and knew that he fully understood the extent of her offer.

• • •

Walter Evans, a pharmacist and the owner of the vandalized drug store on Washington Street, was known for providing briskly efficient service with a pleasant demeanor. However, that demeanor evaporated with his broken window. Over the 27 years that he had owned the pharmacy, his windows had survived huge crowds celebrating sports victories and even the occasional street brawl. But, now he had to go to the trouble and expense of calling a glazier because of an act that was as pointless as it was malicious. Of course, the police would take a report but he, like other downtown merchants, had already gotten the message that the occupiers had the blessing of Town Hall and the police department had to take its cues from the Mayor and the Town Manager.

While calls to Town Hall fell on deaf ears, he got a chance to vent about the broken window the next day while running an errand to St. Paul's. While in the church office, he saw that the door to Reverend Jimmy's study was open. He poked his head in the door.

"Jimmy, those damn occupier kids broke one of my windows while they were destroying Washington Street yesterday. I know you want to let them use the church, but do you think that was really a good idea?"

"I heard about the vandalism, Walter. That's really terrible," Jimmy said softly. "But, we don't even know that the people responsible for the vandalism were occupiers. They could have been troublemakers who just wanted to make the occupiers look bad. For all we know, the people wearing the masks were some bored frat boys."

"I don't know, Jimmy," Walter countered. "These kids just set up camp in the middle of town without permission. It doesn't seem like much of a stretch from that to breaking windows and spray painting the bank."

"Walter, I know some of these kids and they are not troublemakers or vandals. They're a good bunch." He paused and added, "In fact, I am going to be putting my money where my mouth is and spending a night camping with them over at the Plaza. If they weren't decent kids, I doubt they would want a middle-aged minister hanging around."

• • •

Linda picked up the *Morgan Springs News* from her driveway. She immediately looked at a front page article, under Jennifer Harper's byline, which reported on the protest at AmeriBank. The article was accompanied by a picture of the occupiers, prior to donning their masks, marching in an orderly line down Washington Street. The title of the article read "AmeriBank Challenged by Mostly Peaceful Protest."

Linda began to read. Jennifer's article described the march from Freedom Plaza and included Michael's description of how AmeriBank was responsible for harming average Americans. For balance, Jennifer included the bank manager's complaints about the protesters toward the end of the article. The article did not mention what the manager found by the ATM machine even though he had provided Jennifer with details.

The article addressed the vandalism in the next to the last paragraph of the story. Linda learned that "windows were smashed" and an "ATM was spray painted" after the "mostly peaceful" protest. The description of the events in passive voice gave the impression that the buildings may well have vandalized themselves. Michael was quoted as blaming the vandalism on *agents provocateurs* who infiltrated OMS and used the protest as an opportunity to cause trouble. He also pointed out that the vandalism occurred after the protest officially ended as evidence that OMS was not culpable. The *News* did not include any pictures of the aftermath.

Linda started to think about what had occurred on Washington Street and how it was being portrayed. She accepted the assertion that the window smashers and spray painters were only a minority of the occupiers (if they actually were occupiers). But, she was not comfortable with what had taken place. The *News* article had described the march and protest as "mostly peaceful" but, during most days on Washington Street, things were entirely peaceful. Years had gone by where nothing like this happened. She had learned that, when an article described an event as "mostly peaceful," it was a code for "there was violence or mayhem." She never heard of a church picnic or a Rotary Club meeting described as "mostly peaceful." It was easy to simply paper this over. The excrement could be cleaned up, the spray paint removed, the broken glass swept up, and the windows replaced. In fact, there was no trace of this attack 48 hours later. But Linda began to wonder what type of community Morgan Springs would become if more people behaved this way or if this was a routine occurrence.

The incident at AmeriBank was the hot topic on Morgan Springs' most popular political blog, the Morgan Springs Political Junkie. Like the town itself, the blog was politically left of center and served as an electronic forum for Morgan Springs' political spectators. The blog owner, who spent a lot of time hanging out with OMS in Freedom Plaza, was fully supportive of the occupier protest in front of the bank and provided an account of the action complete with pictures. Like the *News*, the blog did not manage to include any pictures of the damage to the Washington Street businesses. After only a few hours, the blog entry had already attracted scores of comments. Linda began to read them in chronological order.

The first seventeen comments were all supportive of the protest. Several of the commenters appeared to have been participants and discussed the importance of having "sent a message to Wall Street" and how much fun they had temporarily shutting down the bank. Although one commenter boasted about how he "dropped a deuce" in front of the bank's ATM machine, there was no other mention of damage to the bank or nearby businesses.

The eighteenth comment, however, deviated from the general celebratory and supportive tone of the previous comments. Linda thought she recognized the commenter "JuliaM" as one of her neighbors, Julia Mendaris. Julia described herself as sympathetic to Occupy Morgan Springs, but reminded her fellow commenters that they were "praising mob behavior" and giving a free pass to those "who vandalized the downtown area, terrorized people, and disrupted businesses."

In light of what had happened, Julia's post did not strike Linda as unreasonable and she began to think about what she could add to support Julia's point. She began to read through the remaining comments and saw that many were directed at Julia, with some of them being vicious. One commenter suggested that Julia should stay off of the blog since she was a "clueless teabagger" for "siding with Wall Street instead of Main Street." Another called her a "pro-Wall Street fascist."

Linda continued to read and saw that Julia tried to defend herself and explain that she was on board with OMS. But, it was too late. The online mob had a fresh victim and the tone of the discussion began to deteriorate quickly. One commenter sneered, "OMS is about smashing paradigms, lady. If you have a problem with smashing a few windows, we don't need you." One of the more civil commenters asked, "Don't you have better things to do? Pilates class? Making cookies for a bake sale? Picking up your kids from soccer practice?" But otherwise, the anger in the comments seemed to grow as Linda scrolled down as if each commenter was trying to be more outraged by Julia's heresy than the previous one.

Linda thought that her neighbor had made a completely valid point and thought the attacks on her were not only unfair, but also unnecessarily harsh. But, given the severe backlash to Julia's comment, Linda was not about to enter this maelstrom by saying something even mildly supportive of her neighbor. She felt a little bit guilty about not coming to Julia's defense, but decided that this was not the time to get involved.

X

Pete had spent the evening at Freedom Plaza hanging out with a female drama major from the University. For almost two hours, he shared his observations about the screwed up nature of the world, as well as some weed and a six-pack of Pabst Blue Ribbon, with the attractive sophomore. She seemed genuinely interested in his solutions to the world's woes. Pete interpreted her rapt attention as attraction. He was certainly attracted to her and he decided it was time to make his move.

"It's been great talking with you. You really understand what's going on . . . better than anyone I have talked to since we started OMS," he flattered. "I think I could talk with you for, like, hours, but it's getting cold. I think we should continue our, uh, discussion, in my tent," he proposed with the best come-hither look he could conjure.

Her laughter was quick and cruel. Pete knew immediately that the laugh did not come from nervousness or embarrassment, but pure contempt.

"I don't think so," she added with a mocking smile. "I'd better get back to my dorm."

Stunned and humiliated, he watched her leave Freedom Plaza and cross Washington Street. He quickly drained the remaining half of his beer, crushed the aluminum can, and flung it in frustration. Now that the investment of his time, marijuana, and beer was not going to pay off, Pete decided to take the two block walk to the bathroom facilities at St. Paul's and grab a shower. As he walked along Washington Street, he fumed that he had wasted a fair amount of some choice dope only to get blown off. The night air was quite brisk now, but his anger did not cool as he walked. He passed a large magnolia tree and the church's neoclassical façade came into view. Pete could see that the parking lot alongside the church was almost empty. During a previous visit to St. Paul's, Pete had been surprised at the level of activity in the church during the evening and learned that the church was used for a wide range of church-affiliated and community organizations. But tonight, it appeared that this was a light evening for meetings or any meetings had already concluded.

Pete walked into the side entrance of the church's main building and entered a hallway. As he entered, he passed a high school girl who had been attending a Girl Scout meeting. Noticing the glazed look on his face, she eyed him warily as she exited.

Pete needed to go deep into the building to get to the shower. However, as he walked down the hall, he was drawn to a light coming from the far side of the church's "Fellowship Hall." He entered what turned out to be the church kitchen and saw, on one of the kitchen counters, the remnants of a cake left over from the Girl Scout meeting. The Girl Scouts had assumed that church employees or others using the church kitchen might finish it off the next day.

The Girl Scouts were certainly correct that it would not go to waste. Pete's brain was under the influence of the tetrahydrocannabinol, or THC, from the pot he had been smoking. It was as if the cake was calling his name. He found a knife and helped himself to a large, square piece of the sugary cake. After finishing the cake, Pete spied a large, warehouse club sized plastic tub of pretzels and helped himself to several handfuls. With his THC-induced cravings satisfied by this carbohydrate fix, Pete decided that organized religion might not be such a bad thing after all.

While Pete was helping himself to a snack in the church kitchen, the Girl Scout, Megan Gray, was waiting in the parking lot for her ride home. It was now 25 minutes past the end of her meeting and she was growing increasingly frustrated since she still had homework to do. Her frustration was compounded by the fact that the battery in her cell phone was dead so she could not call home to see when she could expect to get picked up. She walked back into the church building to see if she could find someone with a cell phone.

As she entered the Fellowship Hall, she saw Pete coming out of the kitchen. Because Pete had been raiding the kitchen rather than using the bathroom facilities, he felt sheepish and wondered if the girl would say something. However, Megan was too annoyed about not having a ride home to ask Pete why he was in the kitchen.

"Excuse me, but do you have a phone I could borrow?" she asked.

Pete's concerns about being busted for foraging in the kitchen dissolved and he had a sudden feeling of power. She needed something from him and he decided to press his advantage.

"I might," he said coolly. "What's in it for me? What are you going to give me to make it worth my while?" he asked with a leer.

Megan's expression changed immediately. Despite his alcohol and THC-clouded judgment, he immediately interpreted a look of disgust. Who was this snotty little bitch to look at him like that? His anger, at a low boil from the time he left Freedom Plaza, suddenly overwhelmed him. He reached out to grab her. His hand touched her wrist but she jerked it away before he could get a firm grip. Megan turned and ran from the dining room. Pete took off after her.

Megan had grown up in St. Paul's and had spent much of her childhood in this building. Over the years, she had learned its labyrinth-like hallways from many games of hide and seek and capture the flag. But, this was no game. Megan would have to use her knowledge of the building to outwit and get away from this unknown predator. She remembered that a large classroom in the basement had an emergency exit to the outside. Better yet, the exit was alarmed and the alarm would be triggered if anyone opened the door. She entered the stairwell to the basement pulling the door closed behind her to impede her pursuer.

Arriving at the basement level, Megan slammed the door at the bottom of the stairwell shut and raced down the hall toward the large classroom at the end. As she entered the classroom, she was horrified to see that the emergency exit had been blocked with a Boy Scout troop's paraphernalia and camping equipment. The troop had been cleaning out and reordering their storage room and had left their gear out. Megan knew she could never pull their mess out of the way before the creep from the kitchen caught up with her. She instinctively grabbed the first thing she could find that looked like it could be used as a weapon.

The Boy Scouts, along with their other gear, had left their flagpoles out. One was used for the American flag and topped with a metal bald eagle. The other was used for their troop flag and was topped with a metal fleur-de-lis, the symbol of the organization. This metal fleur-de-lis came to a point which made the flagpole a spear of sorts, albeit not a particularly deadly one.

Pete entered the large classroom at the end of the hallway just as Megan was grabbing the flagpole spear.

He cautiously closed the distance between himself and Megan thinking about his next move.

Megan had attended the church for her entire life and had spent three years in its junior choir. She had learned that there were certain things you did not say in church. But, her instincts for self-preservation kicked in and she opted to use the language of her high school peers rather than language that would meet with the approval of her Sunday school teachers.

"Get away from me, asshole," she shouted as loud as she could, pointing the flag pole in Pete's direction. "I will fucking kill you."

Pete stood a few feet away feeling a mixture of anger and confusion. He figured this girl was some privileged and pampered daughter of sanctimonious people who attended this church. He enjoyed the feeling of power he got from her obvious terror. On some level, it was a means of getting back at the college woman who rejected his advances earlier. On another level, it was a means of taking on the powerful in society. It did not occur to him that this teenage girl was wondering if he intended to rape her, kill her, or both.

"Get out, you bastard," she shouted, interrupting his muddled thoughts.

While Pete was trying to sort out his next move, he and Megan heard a sharp tap on a window that faced an alley behind the church. Megan's yelling had attracted the attention of a student who was using the alley as a shortcut between the University library and his dorm. Megan's shouting and her threat to kill Pete had drawn the student to the window and he could clearly see the faceoff in the basement. He was not immediately sure who was the potential attacker and the potential victim, but he wanted to put them on notice that there was a witness.

Between being startled by the tapping on the window and processing the fact that there was now a witness, Pete stared at the window. He squinted trying to make out the student obscured by the reflection off the glass of the basement window from the lights.

Megan saw that Pete was distracted and used the opportunity to full advantage. She lunged forward and jabbed the metal fleur-de-lis into Pete's ribcage as hard as she could. Her purpose was two-fold. She wanted to eliminate the immediate threat Pete posed but, she also wanted the witness to know that she was in danger in the basement. Pete clutched his side and looked up stunned while Megan repositioned for a second thrust. She could tell that she had hurt him and did not know if she should continue the attack or allow him to retreat. Suddenly, she feared that if she poked him again she might be the one getting in trouble.

61

"You bitch!" he shrieked.

"Get out. Now," she countered icily.

Pete turned and shuffled out of the room. As Megan saw him moving down the basement hallway, she shouted to the unseen witness to call 9-1-1, hoping she would be heard. She then decided to climb out the basement window because she was not sure how much she had injured the attacker and whether he would return. Full of adrenaline, Megan pushed a heavy wooden table against the wall under the window, climbed up, and then exited. The student who had interrupted the standoff was already on the phone with the 9-1-1 dispatcher.

XI

Pete lumbered down the brick sidewalk of Washington Street clutching his left side. He feared that the flagpole spear had penetrated his skin. Stopping under a streetlight, he pulled up his shirt to examine himself. To his relief, there was no blood, but he was developing a very large and nasty bruise. He wondered if his ribs were broken. He decided the best course of action was to get back to his tent and disappear for the night. Maybe the whole incident at St. Paul's would just blow over. Once he arrived back at Freedom Plaza, he quickly said "goodnight" to Michael and a huddle of several other occupiers and climbed into his small backpacking tent with difficulty. With each movement, he felt the pain from his injury increasing.

Meanwhile, Megan and the student witness gave a report to a University security officer and then, Sergeant Douglass Epps, of the Morgan Springs Police Department. Megan described Pete, his behavior, clothing, and her impression that he was probably drunk or on drugs. At this point, Epps believed that he knew where he might find her attacker. Sometimes, random homeless people would wander into churches or University buildings, but they were rarely aggressive and usually did not sport clothing with political messages. This attacker sounded very much like a young man Epps had become acquainted with at Freedom Plaza; an occupier who had frequently used the lax enforcement of the regulations at Freedom Plaza to flaunt local marijuana laws. Epps knew exactly where his next stop would be after he finished taking Megan's report.

Twenty minutes later, the rotating blue lights of two Morgan Springs Police Department cruisers were slashing at the tents in Freedom Plaza. Sergeant Epps and three other officers exited the vehicles and walked up to several occupiers who were hanging out and chatting. They thought they saw a couple of the campers secreting beer bottles as they approached, but Epps and the other patrolmen had a far more serious issue to deal with than open container violations.

"Which one of you is the leader?" Epps asked as he approached.

"Here," Michael answered raising his hand. "I'm Michael. What can I do for you?"

"I need to talk with one of your comrades. The one wearing a shirt with Che Guevara on it. Is he here?"

Michael, of course, knew immediately who the policeman was asking about.

"Sounds like Pete. What's going on? Why do you want him?" Michael countered trying to assert some authority. "If you think he has done something wrong, you might want to talk to Marcus. He's in charge of security and safety here in Freedom Plaza."

Epps could not believe the audacity of this kid. "Son, Marcus, whoever the hell he is, isn't in charge of a damn thing. I'm in charge and I'm looking for a guy wearing a grimy white tee shirt with Che on it. Now, Michael, I need you to kindly tell me which one of these tents houses the shitbird I'm looking for. Or, I'm gonna pull everyone out of every tent until I find him."

Epps locked his eyes on Michael, forcing him to make the next move. Michael realized that he had to give Epps what he wanted.

Michael walked over to Pete's tent, with Epps following.

"Hey Pete, there's someone from the police department who needs to talk with you."

Pete was awake and had heard the entire conversation between Epps and Michael. He began to panic and tried to play for time.

"What do you want, man? I'm trying to sleep."

Michael was about to answer when Epps cut in. "I need you to come out, son. I need you to come out . . . now."

Pete realized he had no choice. "Okay, okay, just a minute," he whined as he pulled on a sweatshirt. It was too late to get rid of his dope but, with increasing dread, he sensed that getting busted with a little pot was probably the least of his worries. He crawled out of the tent awkwardly and Epps noted that Pete's difficulty might have been due to the injury from his encounter with Megan.

"What's up?" Pete asked.

"Where have you been this evening, Pete?" Epps asked flatly.

"Oh, just around here, for the most part," Pete answered truthfully but incompletely.

"Have you been over to St. Paul's?" Epps prodded helpfully.

"Uh, yeah. I went there to go to the bathroom. They said we could use their bathrooms," he explained.

Epps nodded. "Did you, by any chance, see anyone there?" he asked with a tone of rising irritation.

"Okay," Pete responded. "I don't know what that little bitch told you, but I didn't do anything to her."

"Sounds like you didn't get a chance. You're lucky she didn't kill you," Epps added sarcastically.

Pete knew he had nothing else to say. He assumed that the cop had talked to the girl in the church as well as the witness outside the basement window. It was time to shut up and find a lawyer, he realized.

Epps told him "You're going to be camping with us tonight, Pete. The good news is we've got a cell that's a little bigger than your tent."

As Pete was led away from Freedom Plaza to Epp's patrol car, he briefly thought that a show of defiance might be in order. Then, something told him he should not make trouble for an African-American cop. "Oh man," Pete thought, "if this cop were white I would go off on him and speak some truth to power." But, in Pete's mind, Epps was a victim, just like Pete. The policeman just had not figured it out yet. Pete thought Epps probably naively believed that he had a real chance for career advancement in the MSPD. But, Pete guessed, the cop would eventually learn that he was an exploited tool, the hired muscle of the One Percent.

Pete almost felt sorry for him.

Epps, on the other hand, did not feel sorry for himself or think of himself as a victim. He also did not waste his time on some psycho-social analysis of what Pete thought or why Pete did what he did. He simply thought that Pete was an overly indulged, upper-middle class punk who desperately needed to have his ass kicked.

• • •

During its first couple of weeks, Occupy Morgan Springs had been flying high. The occupation had been getting lots of favorable press coverage. Several hundred people were showing up for the evening meetings every night. Michael and Katie and some of the more flamboyant occupiers had become local celebrities. Many in the community would discuss their visits to Freedom Plaza on Facebook as they might discuss the opening night of the latest blockbuster film, an important football game, or a major rock concert. Even the mess at AmeriBank had been smoothed over and attributed to the youthful overzealousness of a small minority.

But, despite all the indulgence and goodwill that Occupy Morgan Springs enjoyed, Michael and Katie realized that the Pete incident at St. Paul's could put some real heat on them. Megan Gray's father was furious and raising hell with the Mayor, the Town

Manager, the Chief of Police, Reverend Jimmy, and anyone else who would listen.

The Pete situation could also present problems beyond the angry, protective father. OMS had gone to great lengths to achieve gender balance in its leadership and address the concerns of community and campus feminists. Michael and Katie were presented to the public as co-leaders of the occupation. After taking over Freedom Plaza, the occupiers designated it as a VAW-free zone (VAW being an acronym for "Violence Against Women"). Katie had boasted that a woman sleeping in a tent in Freedom Plaza was safer than women in the "rape friendly environment" of the campus and its dorms. Given all the attempts to present themselves as attentive to gender issues, Pete's attack on a female, and a teenager, had to be dealt with quickly.

Their first thought was to see if Reverend Jimmy could assist since the unfortunate incident had taken place at St. Paul's and the girl was a member of the church. Maybe he had some pull with the family and could make this go away, or at least reduce the impact. Katie found Reverend Jimmy's name and number in her phone's contact list and called him from Freedom Plaza.

Jimmy was definitely interested in helping. The incident in his church did not reflect well on Occupy Morgan Springs, but it was not good for him either. He had offered the occupiers the use of St. Paul's facilities without consulting the church's lay committee. Several members of the congregation had already expressed concern and even outright disapproval of letting the occupiers use the facilities. Now, he would have to take the heat for the alleged assault of a child on church property.

"I'll call the girl's parents for you and see what I can do," Jimmy offered as he ended the call with Katie.

Jimmy then found the telephone number of the Grays in the church directory and dialed it. As he heard the ring tone, the pastor prayed that Ms. Gray would answer rather than Megan's father. Jimmy assumed that some members of his congregation were not thrilled to have him as their Senior Pastor, but in the case of Mr. Gray, he knew that to be the case. Megan's mother, Charlotte Gray, on the other hand, had been a lifelong member of St. Paul's and would, hopefully, be more sympathetic.

Jimmy's prayer was answered as he heard Ms. Gray's voice on the other end of the line. "Charlotte, it's Jimmy Dawson. I wanted to let you know how sorry I was to hear about Megan's terrible experience the other night. How is she doing?" he began.

"Thank you for calling. She was pretty shaken up, as you can imagine. She hasn't been sleeping very well. Of course, it could have been much worse, so we are thankful for that."

After expressing his concern, Jimmy moved to the delicate plea for leniency for Pete.

"You know, the young man, Peter Vaughn, who your daughter had the run in with, is a pretty troubled kid. I understand he had been smoking marijuana and drinking . . . probably didn't know what he was doing. From what I understand, he doesn't have a criminal record or history of causing problems. He seems like a kid who just had a serious lapse of judgment. I think what happened could be summed up mostly as a misunderstanding."

Jimmy was hoping for agreement or at least acknowledgment that Charlotte had heard him. But, he got only silence. Charlotte thought she knew where Jimmy was trying to take the conversation and she wasn't inclined to give him any help. His discomfort was palpable.

"So, as your pastor," Jimmy continued to break the too-long silence, "I was hoping I could prevail upon you and David, and Megan of course, to show this troubled young man some forgiveness. He is just a kid and we don't want to ruin his life over one stupid mistake."

After a few uncomfortable seconds, Jimmy heard an audible sigh on the other end.

"Reverend Dawson, David and I are not big fans of cheap grace. It's hard enough to offer some blanket forgiveness to this man – he is not just some kid, by the way – this man, who grabbed our daughter, chased her through a church, terrorized her, and was probably going to rape her or worse. But, where is his contrition? You're the one calling us, not him. Does he even understand that he's done something wrong? Do you actually know if he is sorry for what he did? Does he even want our forgiveness?"

Clearly, there would be no leniency for Pete from the Gray household. Jimmy was resigned to defeat so he moved to end the call as quickly as possible.

"I understand. I know it was a lot to ask of you. Again, I can see why you are angry with Peter."

But, although Jimmy was finished with the conversation, Ms. Gray was not yet finished with her pastor. Revered Jimmy would have to wait a bit longer for a merciful end to this call.

"I'm not just angry at Megan's attacker. I was not too thrilled to learn that you put out the welcome mat for this man and his friends so they could have free rein of the church. You had no idea who they were or what type of people they were."

"They are a group of idealistic people who are working for social justice. They are peacefully protesting what they see as the tremendous wrongs in our society," Jimmy said in his defense.

"I think Megan would disagree with you about the 'peaceful' part," she countered. "I think it has become pretty clear that they should never have been allowed to run amok in our church."

"Part of our church's mission is to be welcoming to people. We don't want to be judgmental," he protested.

"You know, the root word of 'judgmental' is 'judgment.' If you had used good judgment in the first place, this never would have happened. How many of them do you actually know? How many of them are even from Morgan Springs? They had no qualms about occupying the Plaza. They just moved in and took it over. What if they decided to occupy St. Pauls? What if they wanted to sleep and smoke pot and drink beer and have sex and urinate in our sanctuary – or your newly remodeled office?"

Jimmy wanted out of this conversation as quickly as possible.

"I know I've taken enough of your time, Charlotte. Again, I'm sorry this all happened and I hope Megan is okay."

As Jimmy hung up, he wondered if he might have been better off talking to Mr. Gray, or even Megan. There was one thing he was pretty sure of. The Grays would not be increasing their annual pledge for the upcoming year.

Jimmy called Katie to give her the bad news. He was sent to her voice mail where he left a brief message. "The Grays are not budging. They want to crucify Peter. I'm sorry I couldn't help."

• • •

Katie wanted to make sure Jennifer got OMS' official position on the Pete incident for the next edition of the *News*. Although Pete had been the de facto librarian of the Occupation and had been hanging around from the first morning, he would have to be airbrushed out of the picture. Katie had a prepared statement to give to Jennifer.

"Occupy Morgan Springs is part of a national movement which represents 99 percent of Americans and its message has attracted a diverse group of people. Our camp in Freedom Plaza seeks to be a model for the larger Occupy movement throughout the country. We welcome people of all races, religions, sexual identities, social classes, and political ideologies. Unfortunately, while the vast majority of movement participants are law abiding, well intentioned, and thoughtful idealists who seek to build a better society, there is a small minority of individuals who abuse our openness, tolerance, and generosity. The individual recently arrested in connection with the incident at St. Paul's Church was not, in any way, representative of our movement or its principles and goals. He is not associated with Occupy Morgan Springs."

At this point, Jennifer Harper was very easy to find. She had spent time in Freedom Plaza since the occupation began but, at this point, she was more than a mere observer. Michael decided to take her up on her offer of "anything" and she was now spending at least one-half of her nights in his tent.

Over the past couple of weeks, Jennifer had seen and spoken with Pete on many occasions. The assertion that he was not part of Occupy Morgan Springs was ludicrous. However, the statement Katie created was worded to say that Pete "is" not part of the movement, which was technically accurate since Pete was currently in jail and wasn't coming back to Freedom Plaza anytime soon. In Jennifer's rationalization, he did not represent the vast majority of the people in Freedom Plaza. Pete was an outlier and he should not be allowed to harm the reputation of the rest of the group. She had no problem supporting the official line that Pete was not really part of OMS.

She began to craft her next article for the *News*.

XII

Some in Morgan Springs who were inconvenienced by or concerned about the occupation of Freedom Plaza tried to contact Bill Wingate, the Town Manager, to complain. He had devised and perfected several strategies for avoiding them. If called, his office would refer people to the Mayor's Office or the Police Department or promise to get back with the caller "shortly." Anyone who would stop by his office at Town Hall would learn from the receptionist that Wingate was booked up for the day. After work, he could escape quickly out a side entrance that put him only 20 feet from his designated parking space.

Wingate's luck finally ran out at the supermarket when, because his wife was out of town, he had to do the household grocery shopping. As he was searching the unfamiliar aisles for specific items and brands from a long list his wife provided, he was spotted by Burke Thornton.

Burke was not comfortable waylaying public officials outside of work. He believed that they were entitled to some semblance of normal life and privacy. But Wingate, like the Mayor, had been avoiding OMS critics and refusing to respond to their calls or emails. Under the circumstances, Burke decided that it was not unreasonable to "bump" into Wingate and try to strike up a neighborly conversation. He wondered if he, or anyone else for that matter, would get another chance to talk with the elusive Town Manager. He watched Wingate leave the dairy section and, when the Town Manager chose a checkout lane, Burke pulled his own cart behind him to trap him. The shopper in front of Wingate had a full cart so there would be enough time for a brief chat.

"Hello, Mr. Wingate, I'm Burke Thornton."

Wingate turned to Burke with the expression of a deer.

"Hello. Nice to meet you," he lied.

"Nice to meet you, too. I have a question about the OMS folks in Freedom Plaza."

"Sure," Wingate responded warily.

"They've been there for a while now. I'm curious. How is it that they are camping there when Plaza regulations don't allow overnight stays and structures?"

Wingate began to regret his choice of checkout lane. He decided his first recourse would be to argue civic virtue and pride. "Well, Morgan Springs is a town where people like to speak out. Free speech is a community value that the Mayor and Town Council want to support. It sets us apart from other communities."

"I see," Burke countered, "but their freedom of speech is crowding out the freedom of speech of other groups. What about the groups who signed up in advance to use the Plaza for fundraisers? What about anyone who is not part of that group who would like to set foot on the Plaza? It's packed with tents. I thought the regulations were designed to make sure no one monopolized the Plaza."

"Yeah, well we're still in the process of clarifying our policy."

"It certainly needs clarification. Last year, after the Town Council approved the new algorithm for calculating property taxes, a group of eight or nine people assembled in the Plaza to protest the Council's decision. It took only 20 minutes for the police to get there and move them out. They sent four police cars. That's more than you would get for a murder!"

"That group didn't follow the regulations. They set up a structure," Wingate said dismissively.

"The 'structure' was a large cardboard box that they used as a prop – a symbol of an excessively taxed home. No one planned to actually live in that box in Freedom Plaza for weeks."

"Also, there was concern that the protesters might be violent," Wingate continued, starting to sound more indignant. "People who complain about taxes are often anti-government extremists. We were afraid they might be armed. After all, those are the kind of people who seem to love their guns."

Burke had heard enough. He was tired of the Town Manager's weaseling.

"Mr. Wingate, the occupiers are there because you want them to be. If Freedom Plaza had been taken over by a church group or Boy Scouts, they wouldn't have lasted any longer than those tax protesters last year. You and the Mayor have turned Morgan Springs into Orwell's *Animal Farm* where 'some animals are more equal than others.'"

Wingate was speechless. He was relieved when the uncomfortable silence was interrupted by the checkout clerk asking him if he had a customer loyalty card.

• • •

Linda entered the Healthy Planet Market to shop for the evening's dinner. Needing only a few items, she picked up a hand basket and headed toward the produce section in search of salad greens. She saw her neighbor Julia selecting lemons from a citrus bin and they made eye contact. After the beating Julia endured on the Morgan Springs Political Junkie blog a few days earlier, Linda almost expected her to appear bruised and disheveled. Linda walked toward Julia and they exchanged greetings.

Linda had to carefully think out her approach to the next topic. "I have to say Julia, I was appalled at the garbage people were writing on the Political Junkie. I was browsing this morning, and could not believe the awful things people wrote in response to what you said. You sounded perfectly reasonable to me."

Linda had, of course, watched Julia get bludgeoned on the blog in real time. She was too embarrassed to admit that she had remained silent while watching the online pack tear her friend to pieces.

"Yeah, that blog is a real zoo," Julia responded while rolling her eyes upward. "I don't know why they don't get it that I'm not the enemy. What do you have to say? What do you have to do?"

• • •

Reverend Jimmy had decided that it was time to make good on his promise to show solidarity with OMS and camp with the occupiers. He arrived at Freedom Plaza around 10 o'clock after eating dinner with his family, answering some emails, and gathering a sleeping bag and other gear. His tent mate would be Jerry Grant, a middle aged activist he had known for over 20 years. While the youngsters tended to hang out and chat late into the evening, Jimmy was already feeling cold and wanted to go to bed to get out of the cold air. Jennifer Harper was on hand to take a photo of Jimmy crouching down to enter the two-man tent. Her stories had featured some "celebrity" occupiers who had spent the night in Freedom Plaza – a member of the Town Council, a Romance Languages professor from the University, a "between projects" B-movie actor who hailed from Morgan Springs – and Jimmy figured his photo might appear in the next issue of the *Morgan Springs News*. After sliding into the sleeping bag, he texted a "goodnight" message to his wife. Despite the low buzz of youthful conversation outside of his tent, he was able to fall asleep quickly.

A few hours later, Jimmy woke from a strange and disconcerting dream. After a few seconds, he remembered that he was in a tent at Freedom Plaza and not in his own bed at home. He felt quite cold and realized he had brought one of the family's lighter weight sleeping bags by mistake. His misery was compounded by the fact that his high tech camping mattress did not sufficiently pad him from the concrete of the Plaza. Jimmy realized that he might be a lot happier on the couch in his office at the church. It was only two blocks away. He could also have a nice, hot shower in the morning. Besides, he already had his photo op so there was nothing more to be gained by being uncomfortable, cold, and miserable.

Working in the small space of the tent, and trying to avoid waking Jerry, Jimmy awkwardly pulled on his jeans. After slipping on his coat, he unzipped the tent opening, found his shoes, and put his feet through the tent door to exit carefully and quietly. He hoped the youngsters who had been hanging out earlier had gone to bed themselves so no one would witness his escape.

Jerry was awakened by either the cold draft or Jimmy's movement.

"Jimmy? Everything okay?" he mumbled.

"Yeah. Something just came up and I've got to get over to the church," he whispered.

"What is it? What's wrong?" Jerry asked, becoming a bit more alert.

"Oh, nothing serious, " Jimmy responded comfortingly. "I just need to get over there for a bit. I'll see you in the morning."

Jimmy emerged from the cold, miserable tent into the clear, starry fall night. Fortunately, there was no one outside to catch him sneaking off. He thought he might try to find some way to return later to make an appearance in the morning, but he also realized it would only get colder in the next few hours. He hoped the lie he told Jerry would cover him and leave his reputation as Morgan Springs' leading clergy activist untarnished. As he walked toward his church and its promise of greater warmth and comfort, what was left of any sense of shame quickly vanished.

· · ·

Linda woke earlier than usual. She had been following the latest OMS developments on the Political Junkie blog and other websites just before going to bed the previous night. The different sources provided a swirl of conflicting rumors about someone in OMS attacking a girl at a downtown church. Perhaps, she thought, the latest edition of the *Morgan Springs News* would provide some clarity and set the record straight.

She loaded ground coffee into the filter of her drip coffeemaker, turned it on, and wandered outside to pick up the newspapers from the end of her driveway. Surprisingly, the temperature had dropped more than expected overnight and Linda realized her house slippers and terrycloth robe would do little to ward off the freezing temperatures. She moved quickly to retrieve the papers and get back inside.

Coffee now in hand, Linda sat down at her breakfast table with the *Morgan Springs News* and saw that there was an article about the occupation on the first page. The article, with Jennifer Harper's byline, was entitled "Occupiers Face Challenges as They Build a New World." The article discussed a range of issues faced by the occupiers such as acquiring funds for their operations, assigning responsibilities in the camp, ensuring a safe environment for female and transgendered occupiers, arriving at a consensus in disputes, and determining OMS' next steps. Linda turned to the inside of the paper where the lengthy article continued. Toward the end of the article, almost as an afterthought, Jennifer mentioned another "challenge" for OMS: what to do about occupiers (or alleged occupiers) who commit crimes. It was here that the incident at St. Paul's was finally addressed.

The article pointed out that Peter Vaughn, who sometimes hung out at the OMS camp in Freedom Plaza, was arrested for assault. Jennifer dutifully included the full statement crafted by Katie which denied that Peter Vaughn had any role in OMS. For good measure, she added a quote from Michael where he complained that detractors were trying to use isolated incidents and the behavior of a few wayward individuals to damage OMS' reputation. Apparently, in addition to Megan Gray, OMS was one of Peter Vaughn's victims.

Linda wondered if the Peter Vaughn mentioned was the Pete she met at the "People's Library" on the first day of the occupation. Later, when at her computer, she checked out the MSPD online police blotter and saw Pete/Peter's mug shot and the details of his arrest and alleged crime.

• • •

Reverend Jimmy woke up on the couch in his 70 degree office a few hours after his sudden disappearance from his tent. Although he did not realize it at the time, he was not missed at Freedom Plaza. His reputation as Morgan Springs' leading clergy activist was secure. Jerry Grant, his tent mate, relayed Jimmy's cover story to the other occupiers and the general assumption was that Jimmy was helping a bereaved church member or otherwise doing God's work over at St. Paul's.

There was another reason that the occupiers did not spend any time thinking about Jimmy's absence. Like Jimmy, many of the occupiers also had had a very cold and miserable night. During the first days of the occupation, the mild nights had made camping out in Freedom Plaza not only tolerable, but also fun. But, the first truly cold night had brought home the reality that winter was coming. Despite the braggadocio about digging in and staying at Freedom Plaza as long as necessary, a long winter of Valley Forge-like stoicism was just not realistic. Even though winters in recent years had been relatively mild, the occupiers would have to expect temperatures in the teens or even single digits. Add some high winds, significant snowfall, or an ice storm and you would have tremendous misery, probable illness, and possibly even death.

If OMS wanted to keep the occupation going past November, they would need to occupy someplace warmer. It was time for Occupy Morgan Springs to enter a new phase.

XIII

Early the next Saturday morning, the Morgan Springs Police Department received a call reporting unusual activity around the old Tabor's Variety Store building, a two story, red-brick structure which had closed its doors a decade before. From time to time, a homeless person might get in to bed down for the night. But, the caller indicated that, rather than one or two trespassers, there might be as many as two or three dozen people in the building. Based on reports of occupier activity and tactics from other cities around the country, the Police Department deduced that the trespassers in the building were part of Occupy Morgan Springs.

Douglass Epps and another policeman went to the Tabor's building to investigate. The front door was securely locked and did not appear to have been disturbed. They saw a manifesto taped to the door that announced the occupation of the building "in the name of the 99%." The document declared that "The People" had determined that the building's owner, Gene Baskin (presumably a member of the One Percent) had "lost any and all rights to the building because it was not being used for the benefit of the community." The manifesto went on to promise that the building would be repurposed as a day care center, homeless shelter, food pantry, and community education center.

The officers had been told that people had been getting in through a rear entrance so they circled behind the building. They found the rear door slightly ajar and quickly pulled it open. Inside, they saw a young man sweeping the cement floor with a push broom.

"Good morning," Epps said firmly. "I'm Sergeant Douglass Epps of the Morgan Springs Police Department. This is Officer Reid Chandler. Who's the head revolutionary here?"

"I'll get him," the trespasser answered brusquely and walked away.

Epps and Chandler quickly looked around to assess what the trespassers might be doing. There was some evidence that this had been a variety store ten or so years earlier – some rusted shelving and damaged clothing racks – but mostly, they saw evidence of a decade of neglect and abuse. Numerous beer cans, liquor bottles, and fast food bags gave the impression that teenagers and homeless people had been using the building as a hangout for some time. However, most of this litter was piled in one area and whole sections of the floor were swept as if the trespassers had been doing some housekeeping.

Upon examining the cleaner areas, the two policemen saw some things that were disconcerting. There appeared to be 15 or 20 gasoline cans clustered in a corner. They saw eight or ten milk crates filled with rocks. The rocks, each about the size of a very large egg, looked like they would be excellent projectiles. They also saw a large collection of glass bottles. More projectiles? Molotov cocktails?

Epps could not resist the temptation to comment. "Hey, Reid, you think these kids are going to finance their revolution with the deposit money from these bottles?"

There was also evidence that the trespassers were planning to stay for awhile. One space had been set up as a sleeping area with perhaps a dozen sleeping bags on camping mattresses. Another area had stacks of packaged food and gallon jugs of water. The trespassers had even been decorating a little. A banner hung on the wall behind the food storage area said "Viva la Revolucion."

A young, bearded man with close cropped hair walked briskly and cockily up to them. With a faint smile and an arrogant demeanor, he clearly was not the least bit concerned that he was getting a visit from the MSPD. Epps and Chandler quickly understood why. A group of about 20 people had assembled about 40 feet away. They were all wearing dark clothing and had their faces hidden by bandanas or masks. The phalanx of trespassers stood with their arms crossed in a defiant and menacing posture.

"I'm Jonathan, but everyone calls me Fuerza. What brings you here this morning?" he asked with mock affability.

Epps began. "Okay, Mr. Fuerza, we've read your literature about the occupation of this building. I realize that the building is empty and hasn't been used in years, but you are trespassing. You also face a potential charge of breaking and entering. You and your friends need to clear out."

"We're not going anywhere," Fuerza quickly retorted. "We have claimed this unused property in the name of The 99 Percent. Gene Baskin doesn't care about this building and we have far better ideas than he does about what should be done with it. We're going to turn it into a community asset."

Epps suppressed the desire to take his truncheon and knock the smirk off the trespasser's face. He managed to force a smile instead.

"It sounds like you have some really nice plans. Maybe you should share them with Mr. Baskin. But, for now, we have a job to do. Mr. Baskin owns the building and he pays the taxes on it. Unless he wants you here, you are trespassing on his private property. And by the way, I doubt he wants people storing fuel in his building. Why do you have that in here?"

"To run a generator," Fuerza answered.

"I don't see a generator anywhere."

"We have one on the way. Of course, you could turn on the electricity for us."

Epps had had enough of Fuerza's cheekiness. "You need to get out immediately. Like I said, you are subject to arrest for trespassing, breaking and entering, maybe vandalism. You can't save the world from jail."

Fuerza simply shook his head "no," turned away, and walked toward his masked comrades.

One voice from the assembled mob started shouting "ACAB" – the acronym for "All Cops Are Bastards." Almost immediately, he was soon joined by the others chanting in unison.

Chandler and Epps realized that the mob was daring them to do something. It was easy for these cowards to be so bold with a ten-to-one advantage and with their faces covered. The policemen had no idea what weapons they might have at their disposal in addition to rocks and flammable liquids. It was time to leave.

"You don't want to be here when we come back," Epps shouted as they left. The chanting continued and got louder as the policemen exited the building.

• • •

At Freedom Plaza, Michael's iPhone chirped and he could see Mayor Steven Worthington's name flash on the screen. He was not exactly surprised to get the call. He paused briefly to collect his thoughts before answering.

"Good afternoon, Mayor. How are you?" Michael answered cheerily, hoping his tone might reduce the tension.

"Well Michael, I'm not too happy right now. I just got off the phone with my Chief of Police. He said there are occupiers trespassing in the old Tabor's building. What the hell are you people doing?" the Mayor demanded.

"It's not us."

"Then who is it? Is it another Occupy Morgan Springs group I haven't heard of yet? You've got to know about this. Don't tell me you didn't know this was happening."

"Well yeah, I did hear something might be going on over there. But, I swear, we didn't authorize it. We vote on just about everything at our nightly meetings, but we didn't vote on this."

"If you did, you had better hope I never find out. If you know who it is – if you even think you know who it is – you might want to do them a favor and tell them to get out."

Michael got off the phone believing that the Mayor was in the process of cooling off. The Mayor had called him about the windows getting smashed on Washington Street, but that blew over. He also knew that the Mayor despised Gene Baskin and butted heads with him constantly over the underutilized and decrepit properties that Baskin owned in the downtown area. If Worthington let the occupiers stay in Freedom Plaza, he was not going to do anything about the old Tabor's building. After all, he reasoned, kids and homeless people hung out in there all the time and no one ever did anything about it.

The Mayor got off the phone assuming that Michael was not being completely candid with him. But, he at least believed Michael's assertion that the idiots in the building did not represent the larger OMS group. Like the smashed windows on Washington Street, this was about a few loose cannons. That sort of thing happened with these movements. There were always a few people who were either a little too exuberant or who were opportunistic troublemakers who liked to hide in a crowd. He was glad that he could do what needed to be done without running afoul of the saner elements of the OMS crowd.

He dialed the Chief of Police and gave him the green light.

XIV

Four officers from the MSPD returned to the old Tabor's Variety Store Sunday morning to further assess the situation at the building and deliver a final warning to any occupiers who were still present. They found the rear door blocked from inside so that it was possible to open it only about three inches. The trespassers had apparently put something heavy behind the door. An officer called into the opening but got no response. However, they knew occupiers were in the building because it had been under surveillance for hours and the Police Department had kept track of how many people entered and left. He shouted again into the crack.

"We know you are in there. You have an hour to leave. This building will be cleared and everyone in it will be arrested. This is your last chance. Leave now while you can."

Again, there was no response and they turned to leave. As they got back to the street, they caught a glimpse of a young male on the roof peering over the edge. It was Daniel Russo, enjoying his role as sentry as well as the commanding view of downtown Morgan Springs from his perch. He imagined himself manning the battlements of a castle against an invading army. And then, his imagination turned whimsical and he decided to add some levity from one of his favorite movies *Monty Python and the Holy Grail*. "And don't come back or I will taunt you a second time, English pig dogs" he called using his best impression of a British impression of a Frenchman. Amused with his own performance, he burst into laughter.

"Laugh while you can, dipshit," one of the policemen muttered under his breath.

• • •

Several hours later, The Morgan Springs Police Department SWAT team and the Morgan Springs Fire Department set up a command center on University Avenue two blocks from the Tabor's building. Police cars blocked the side streets which intersected with University Avenue. The hope was that the occupiers would get the message when confronted with overwhelming force and leave. The SWAT team leader, Charles Hodges, knew that his men were prepared to resolve situations like this with a frightening level of violence, speed, and efficiency. He did not want to see them demonstrate their full capabilities. And there was another complicating factor. Because the occupiers were believed to be storing gasoline in the building, the situation was, quite literally, potentially explosive and the need for the Fire Department was a disconcerting possibility. Given the circumstances, it was dangerous to use either "flashbang" grenades or tear gas grenades because they had been known to start fires. Hodges silently prayed that the Fire Department trucks would never get closer to the Tabor's building than where they were parked two blocks away.

The imminent raid was starting to draw a crowd of onlookers. Several people, most who appeared to be under 30, were already milling around when the MSPD arrived to set up their command center. Hodges assumed that they were probably occupiers from the Freedom Plaza or OMS groupies, some of whom may have been in the old Tabor's Store. Of course, being outside, they could not be arrested as trespassers, but Hodges assumed they were up to no good.

Knowing something was going down, several bystanders pulled out their phones and began making calls. Hodges assumed that some bystanders were also lookouts who were warning their friends inside the building. That was certainly fine with him. He hoped that the occupiers, upon learning that the MSPD was about to raid the building, would have the good sense to get out. They were going to be removed one way or another so they might as well leave by their own choice and on their feet.

The SWAT team was divided into two groups. The first would start from the command post and move two blocks north to the Tabor's building and gain entry through the front of the building. The other group, starting from two blocks to the north of the building, would move south and force open the rear building entrance which police had found barricaded earlier in the day. Uniformed patrolmen began to clear the street and sidewalks of onlookers as well as put up yellow "caution" tape to create a perimeter. Their job was complicated by the arrival of more spectators who came to see the showdown with the trespassers. Some complained that their civil rights were being violated because they would not be able to see the possible mayhem. However, onlookers managed to find several venues from which to observe the unfolding drama. Hodges wondered if the entire town would show up for the confrontation.

As the two SWAT teams began to approach the occupied building from both the north and the south, the bystanders were quick to display their sympathies. They let out a chorus of jeers and boos as the teams advanced. As more spectators joined, the noise level grew to an impressive level. Despite the consistent roar, the SWAT team members, only minutes away from engaging the trespassers, were completely focused on their task. As loud as the people in the mob became, their vocalizations were reduced to background noise in the mind of each SWAT team member.

As the northbound group moved forward and was one and one-half blocks from the Tabor building, a woman with long gray hair in a single braid emerged from a building. She held a flower in her hand and began to shout at one of the SWAT team members nearest to her on the street.

"Why do you have that machine gun?" she demanded. "Who are we at war with?"

This woman had managed to break through the background noise of the spectators for the SWAT team member. He glanced at the woman and the flower and thought to himself, "Oh man, is this lady for real?"

"Think! Think about what you're doing. You don't have to be a hired killer for the One Percent," the hippy grandmother pleaded.

One of the patrolmen who had helped to clear the street shouted at the woman. "Ma'am, get back inside the building. NOW."

The woman walked quickly along the sidewalk to match the pace of the SWAT team and to avoid the policeman coming toward her. She continued to plead her case to the SWAT member who she had singled out. "Don't do something you'll regret for the rest of your life. Are you really willing to kill these kids?" she whined.

She stepped off the sidewalk to approach the SWAT team member, her hand with the flower outstretched, as if she intended to stick the flower into the barrel of his weapon. At this point the patrolman caught up with her and quickly forced her down to the pavement. As she had been taught in a protesting clinic years before, she began to shriek as if her arms were being ripped off. Her Oscar-worthy performance and mock agony energized the crowd. The policeman pulled her arms behind her back and secured them with plastic handcuffs. As he pulled her up from the street and led her away, the crowd erupted in a mix of cheering for the flower bearer's performance and verbal abuse for the policeman.

The two SWAT groups continued their advance toward the Tabor's building. All of the trespassers had remained in the building so things were going to get ugly very quickly. The crowd of onlookers, energized by the arrest of the flower lady, continued to jeer and shriek at the approaching SWAT teams. Video and photos of the advancing SWAT team were being transmitted with cell phones in real time. The onlookers wanted their friends to know that they had a front row seat at the best show in town.

Hodges and the team had been briefed that the occupiers were stockpiling rocks, and the men approached with this in mind. The leaders kept an eye on the roof line of the two-story building as they slowly advanced along the street from two directions. While the chorus of sympathizers continued to heap verbal abuse on the team, the well-trained members maintained their focus.

The leaders of the two teams continued to watch the roofline for any movement and, as they got within 20 yards, a man's head was spotted.

"Okay, we've got a sentry on the roof," a team leader warned.

Just as he finished his warning, several rocks flew from the roof. Only one of the projectiles came within 10 feet of a team member. Despite the terrible accuracy of the rock throwers, the crowd roared its approval of the trespassers' defensive efforts. The jeering of the SWAT team turned to cheering for the underdogs on the roof.

The SWAT leaders now realized that there were several occupiers on the roof other than the one man who was spotted. Perhaps the sentry they saw was directing the throwing; maybe the rock throwers were getting direction from someone on the ground. Regardless, their accuracy was terrible. Also, each man on the team was wearing a helmet and body armor and was equipped with a shield. Nonetheless, the incompetent rock throwers could still get lucky. The group leaders did not want to run the risk of having their men get hit.

Hodges wanted to get the occupiers off the roof. But, it was just a matter of time before the teams were inside the building. They were now moving along the building walls. The rock throwers, avoiding the edges of the roof, could no longer see the SWAT team members below. The northbound team arrived at the front door and prepared to break in. Simultaneously, the southbound team began their work at the rear entrance.

• • •

Daniel Russo was not overly alarmed to see the wisps of smoke curling out of the roof opening from inside the second floor. Perhaps the SWAT team had thrown smoke grenades or tear gas downstairs. If so, he was better off on the roof. However, Daniel's two comrades decided it might be a good time to leave and they scrambled down the ladder. Daniel, however, was having too much fun on the roof to worry about what might be unfolding inside the building. The old Tabor's building had been turned into a stage and, for the moment, Daniel was the star.

"Daniel," a voice called. Daniel saw one of his comrade's heads poking out of the roof hatch. "We've gotta get out. The building's on fire. Come on."

"Okay," he yelled back.

The smoke coming out of the hatch had become thicker and Daniel moved to the ladder. Because his vision was obscured by the smoke as he descended, he did not realize that his right foot was barely on the rung of the metal ladder. He shifted his weight down seeking a lower rung with his left foot but, before he could find it, his right foot slid from its insecure position. Instantly, his chin smacked against an upper rung and he fell to the floor below. He bit his tongue hard when his chin hit the rung, but he had little time to contemplate the intense pain. His next impact was with the floor below the ladder and he lost consciousness as his mouth began to fill with blood.

• • •

As the SWAT team prepared to push through the back door of the building, they could hear occupiers on the other side of the door frantically pulling away the barricade they had put in place to block the door. With the door slightly ajar, the SWAT team could see and smell smoke. They now understood why the occupiers were desperate to get out. The SWAT members pushed as the occupiers removed the last pieces of the barricade and the door flew open. About a dozen occupiers came out coughing and gagging amid a billowing cloud of acrid smoke. The SWAT team easily collected them as they were too disoriented and frightened to put up any resistance.

The SWAT leader could not be certain that the building was free of potentially hostile individuals, but with a fire in progress, he assumed any remaining trespassers were more likely to be in danger than to be a danger. He radioed the command center to send the fire trucks. Prepared for this contingency, they began to roll toward the burning building in seconds.

The SWAT group leader grabbed Fuerza, the trespasser leader who had been so cocky when Epps and Chandler had visited the previous day.

"We need to know if anyone is still in the building. How many of you were in there?" the SWAT leader asked.

Fuerza stared and blinked, not quite grasping the SWAT leader's greatest fear.

"Think," the SWAT leader prodded. "Is there anyone left in there?"

"There were about a dozen of us or so, I think."

Fuerza, having been able to breathe cleaner air for a few seconds, could recall that, on the previous night, 13 trespassers had decided to stay and hold their ground. He was able to remember because there had been some gallows humor about being "the unlucky 13."

"Twelve of them came out. We have twelve," another SWAT team member interjected.

"Did Daniel get out?" asked one of the rock throwers who had been on the roof.

Fuerza leader looked around again, "Oh my God. Daniel is still in there. He was on the roof watching for you guys."

The firemen would roll up any second but there was no time to lose. Two of the SWAT team members pulled on respirators and prepared to go into the building.

The SWAT leader turned back to Fuerza, "Okay, you've got to help me out. Why is there a fire in there? Did you people set it? We know you had fuel in there. We need to know anything you can tell us about this fire so we can save your friend."

"No, we didn't set it. And there was no gas in the cans," Fuerza responded, still in shock about Daniel's peril. "I don't know how or where it got started. We noticed the smoke and just got out as fast as we could."

"Now," the SWAT leader continued, "are there any booby traps in there? Have you set any traps or do you know of anything in there that poses any additional danger to my men?"

"No, we didn't do anything like that. Please, just hurry and get Daniel out," he pleaded.

The SWAT team had already reviewed blueprints of the store and had noted, based on the report from the previous day, where the trespassers had set up and stored things. They also knew where the hatch to the roof was located on the second floor so they would start searching between the rear entrance and the hatch. The two members wearing respirators entered and immediately disappeared from sight.

Firemen arrived a half a minute later in their turnout gear and entered the building. The jeering and cheering had ended when the spectators, seeing smoke, fire trucks and ambulances, realized that the show across the street had turned into a firefighting and rescue operation. The onlookers did not know exactly what they were watching, or how long the drama would continue, but they knew something had gone terribly wrong in the Tabor's building. They now shared the dread of the SWAT team and firefighters.

The paramedics and SWAT team members outside the rear entrance waited for a two minute eternity before a firefighter emerged with Daniel, limp and bloody. He turned him over to the paramedics who started giving him oxygen.

A few seconds later, the other three rescuers emerged. The second firefighter and one of the SWAT team members were assisting the other SWAT team member who, because his respirator did not work properly, had been overcome by smoke. The SWAT team member would survive, but would probably have respiratory issues for the rest of his life. He would never work on the SWAT team again.

For Daniel, however, it was too late.

XV

News of the tragedy at the Tabor's building spread quickly via the local blogs, Facebook, Twitter, texting and the OMS website. With the spread of this news, came the rapid spread of rumors and distortions, each growing more fantastic by the hour. Morgan Springs was learning that: the SWAT team shot an unarmed Daniel in cold blood; Daniel fell to the sidewalk from the roof of the building; the SWAT team shot other occupiers; the SWAT team started a fire to get the occupiers out of the building; the SWAT team beat up an elderly woman on the street.

By the time the Fire Department had the blaze under control, the hysterical distortions had fueled a campaign to demonize the MSPD as murderers and to elevate Daniel Russo to martyrdom. Jennifer Harper, of course, would write the story for the *Morgan Springs News* but this would not appear until Wednesday as the paper only came out three times a week. However, she could play a role immediately by helping to write the "first draft of history" that would be widely disseminated before anyone read Wednesday's paper. Drawing on her understanding of these types of events, she counseled Michael and Katie to avoid specifics since they could be refuted later. She also told them to leverage the sentiments that the MSPD either did something they should not have done or did not do something they should have done. Finally, she wanted them to play up Daniel's youthful innocence and the senselessness of his death. She knew that once perceptions were established, they would be very difficult to change.

Michael and Katie, with Jennifer's input, began to formulate a communications plan. The first part of the plan was for OMS to categorically deny any involvement in the occupation of the Tabor's building. The trespassers would be described as a radical splinter group which had done its own thing and had not, in any way, taken this action under the auspices of OMS. The second part of the plan, despite the putative lack of any relationship between OMS and the trespassers, was to fit the tragedy into the OMS narrative. The outrageous behavior of the MSPD and Daniel's death would be evidence that Morgan Springs was in the grip of a tiny, but cruel and powerful minority who were bent on controlling the 99 Percent. OMS would wash their hands of the incident at the Tabor's building yet, nonetheless, use it to tell a story of inequality and exploitation.

• • •

Mayor Worthington was already angry about the Tabor's building incident, but became furious when he learned the names of the trespassers who had been arrested. Of the twelve, he immediately recognized five as having been involved in Occupy Morgan Springs in some way. These five, of course, included Daniel Russo, who was rapidly becoming national news.

Steven was especially angry with Michael for lying to him earlier. He now surmised that the people arrested at the Tabor's building had been "colonizing" a new place to occupy for the winter. Freedom Plaza was going to become uninhabitable as the winter set in and OMS had to occupy something else if they wanted to remain viable. The large, abandoned store was a perfect choice.

Steven was also angry with himself for believing Michael's lie about the lack of a link between OMS and the trespassers. But, as he thought about it some more, he realized that his acceptance of Michael's lie was more about his wanting to believe something rather than actually believing it. He had essentially condoned an escalation of OMS' activities. But, before he was able to spend too much time dwelling on his own culpability, he refocused his anger on Michael. Someone was going to have to answer for this fiasco and it certainly wasn't going to be the Mayor. He had a re-election campaign to kick off in a few weeks.

He found Michael's name in his iPhone and angrily stabbed the call button. However, as the number was connecting, Steven had second thoughts and hit the cancel button.

Michael saw the Mayor's name and number briefly appear on his iPhone screen. He was almost certain that Steven was calling to ream him over the disaster at the Tabor's building so he was not sorry to see the call disappear. At the same time, Michael was not so sure he had to be afraid of the Mayor. He and Katie had been assessing the winds of public opinion from the time the ambulances pulled away from the ruined building and they already had a plan for deflecting any heat from OMS.

Steven, equally savvy about public opinion in Morgan Springs, had arrived at the same conclusion as Katie and Michael which is why he cancelled the call to Michael. Instead, he called Bill Wingate, the Town Manager, to arrange a meeting at the Mayor's home as quickly as possible. Wingate had been Town Manager for two years and owed his job to the Mayor. He had been Steven's first choice for Town Manager, but several Town Council members wanted another candidate. The Mayor had resorted to a lot of arm twisting and maneuvering to get Wingate selected. When the occupation of Freedom Plaza began, Wingate thought the logical course of action was to enforce the Plaza regulations and remove the occupiers. However, he had trusted Steven's political instincts and decided not to push back. Now, he feared the Mayor's instincts were going to make Steven a one termer and, with a new Mayor and a couple of changes on the Town Council, Wingate's contract might not be renewed. Wingate needed to put in a few more years as Town Manager to qualify for a sufficient pension. At his age, he was not interested in finding a new job and a move to a new town.

Upon arriving at the Mayor's house, it was clear that Wingate and the Mayor would get down to business immediately. Steven led Wingate to his office after briefly stopping in the kitchen to offer his visitor a beer.

"Steven, we should string up those little bastards," Bill started. "I can't believe they would be so brazen. We gave them the damn Plaza. Wasn't that enough?"

"Bill, I'm as pissed off at them as anyone, but we can't really do anything to them. Not now, anyway."

"Why not?" Bill asked, surprised.

"Well for starters, the occupiers in the Plaza are claiming that they have nothing to do with the people in the Tabor's building. Of course, that's total bullshit, but they might get by with it. Another problem is that we let them stay in the Plaza from the beginning and they have been there for weeks now. If we go after them, we would be admitting we were wrong."

"Steven, people are furious. They are going to have to blame someone."

"You're right Bill. And they've already started. My email is filling up with comments about the police department and the SWAT team."

"So, you are talking about throwing our Police Department under the bus?"

"Not at all. I am talking about the town throwing the Police Department under the bus."

"And we just let them get screwed for doing their job?"

The Mayor had anticipated Wingate's concerns. "Bill, let's look at it this way. I get reelected in May, your job is safe, and we'll do what we can to make things right for the PD after the election."

"Do you think this will fly?"

"I do. I've already read a lot of the emails. Some blame me personally, some have trashed the occupiers, but most people are mad at the Police Department. To begin with, they have some crazy ideas about what really happened. Some of them think the kid was shot by the police, that the police started the fire, lots of other wacko stuff."

"Don't you think people will learn the truth about what really happened?" Bill asked.

"You're assuming they really want to. I think they would prefer to believe the worst. This isn't a town that loves its police, Bill. It just sees them as a necessary evil."

Bill Wingate was beginning to see the logic of the Mayor's reasoning although part of him was appalled at Steven's naked cynicism. The Town Manager's conscience compelled him to play the role of devil's advocate.

"Steven, it might be argued that we should lead and calm people down. Don't you think so?"

"We can create a commission made up of citizens and an alderman to investigate the incident. As Mayor, it would be inappropriate for me to comment one way or another while the commission does its work. I've gotta be neutral or I could bias their work, you see."

"A commission. And how long would this drag out?"

"Well, they need to be thorough. I'm guessing it would take at least six months once the commission was created. Of course, it might take a couple of months to put the commission together."

"They wouldn't be able to report back until the middle of next summer. After the primary."

"Like I said, they need to be thorough."

"Those guys were just doing their job. Do you really think this uproar will continue?"

"You know, Bill, people are freaked out that the PD has the capabilities it has. We've had these types of weapons and teams in place since just after 9/11. But a lot of people in town don't get it that this is really a small city with city issues. They think we live in Mayberry and that our law enforcement is Sheriff Andy Taylor and Deputy Barney Fife armed with revolvers. This has pulled them out of their cocoons and they're shocked to see men in downtown Morgan Springs with big, scary guns. As their Mayor, it is my job to empathize with their shock and fear."

Bill Wingate was astounded at what he was hearing. It left him with a feeling of both awe and horror. He admired the Mayor's political logic and was so focused on Steven's thought processes that he had not even touched his beer.

The Mayor continued, "Another thing to consider is that people aren't happy about the fact that the PD sent in a SWAT team to protect one of those eyesore buildings owned by Gene Baskin. Baskin's an asshole and he's about as popular as gonorrhea. The idea of using force to protect one of his trashy buildings isn't playing very well either. A lot of people think anything the occupiers might have done with the building would have been an improvement.

"Bill, people are confused and angry and they are going to stay confused and angry. And, they'll find new things to be angry about. I'm already seeing the Monday morning quarterbacking in my email. They tell me, 'The police should have given them more chances to leave.' Or 'The police should have just allowed them to stay there for the winter.' I've got no problem with our police department, but they can't win regardless of what we do anyway. This town just has a problem with guns and uniforms.

"It's stupid, Bill. But, that's our way out. The town is going to do our work for us. Sometimes, the best way to be a leader . . . is to simply follow."

Having heard his Mayor's political analysis, Bill Wingate finally took the first swig of his beer.

• • •

Linda first learned about the incident at the Tabor's building while checking her Facebook feed. Her horror at hearing about the death of an 18 year old male was compounded by the realization that he was just one year older than one of her sons and a year younger than the other. She could only imagine what the young man's parents were going through and wondered how she and her husband could carry on if faced with the same tragedy.

Since the onset of the occupation at Freedom Plaza, there had always been some level of online discourse about the OMS. However, with the SWAT involvement, a fire, and a death, the level had become the most intense she had ever seen. She went to the Political Junkie blog and saw that there had been an explosion of comments. There was considerable anger at the MSPD with some comments directed at the Mayor and Town Hall.

As Linda read through the postings and comments, she saw that Julia Mendaris was one of the most prolific contributors. Reading further, she realized that Julia had, in this disaster, found an all consuming mission. Even as the Tabor's fire was still smoldering, Julia was already busy promoting a petition calling for an independent investigation into the "murder" and the "unprovoked police brutality" at the Tabor's building.

Julia's crusade was a bit too precipitous for one blog commenter who suggested that it would be better to move forward with caution, sort out the facts of the incident, and get reports from the MSPD and the Fire Department. But, for many of the blog denizens, this was no time for facts and analysis. Several of the posters went after the errant citizen. Julia's attacks were the most brutal. For Julia, the suggestion that the community should "wait and see" was tantamount to condoning Daniel's death. It was time for action. The naïve commenter was made to pay for his belief in caution.

Linda was impressed with the turnaround in Julia's online fortunes. Only a couple of weeks before, Julia had been a pariah for suggesting that, perhaps, the attack on AmeriBank was not the way of the future. For speaking out, Julia had been punished with a virtual stoning. But, the point of these Political Junkie stonings was not to "kill" the offenders. Rather, the purpose was to bloody them a bit so that they would learn their place. Often, the victims of the last stoning would be the most enthusiastic stone throwers the next time around. For the current spectacle, Julia was now on the outer ring, experiencing catharsis as she bloodied the latest victim.

It had been just two weeks since Julia and Linda had seen each other in the grocery store. At that time, Julia had asked Linda, "What do you have to say? What do you have to do?" Apparently, Julia had learned quickly.

• • •

While Daniel's death was hard on the occupiers, it was especially difficult for Jennifer Harper. With all the time she spent at Freedom Plaza, she had gotten to know him fairly well. Daniel idolized Michael and, in many ways, saw him as an older brother. It was only natural that, once Jennifer started sleeping with Michael, Daniel began to see her as almost a big sister. With Daniel's death, she decided that she would use journalism as an outlet for her grief. Going forward, all her skills and training would be employed to get back at the people responsible for Daniel's death. The coverage of the Tabor's building showdown that appeared in next Wednesday's *News* would be her magnum opus.

Meanwhile, Reverend Jimmy was looking for ways to support the occupation after the tragedy. He hoped that he could have a public memorial service at St. Paul's or perhaps even in Freedom Plaza. However, Daniel's family was still trying to process what had happened. Their understandable grief and confusion were compounded by the fact that they had no awareness of how their son had spent his last few weeks. Daniel was enrolled at the University for the fall semester so they had believed he was taking classes and living in his dorm. In their shock, they had turned to their own pastor. They were not yet ready to respond to any outreach from their son's occupier associates. Jimmy had to be content with the less public role of offering grief counseling to any interested occupiers.

• • •

The next Wednesday, the *Morgan Springs News* appeared with coverage of the story of the year. Jennifer had spared no effort in bringing Morgan Springs all the news fit to print about the incident at the Tabor's building. Fred Hutchinson added his inimitable commentary on what the recent events meant for Morgan Springs and the larger society.

Jennifer dutifully followed Katie and Michael's script. In only the second paragraph, the article stated that the trespassers in the building were not part of Occupy Morgan Springs, but a splinter group acting without the authorization of OMS. Despite the purported lack of any link to the occupiers in Freedom Plaza, it was nonetheless essential to include comments from Michael about the noble goals of the trespassers. Katie was quoted as commenting how the actions of the SWAT team had been the most outrageous use of the police force in town history, and perhaps in state history.

It had been only four days since the masked trespassers in the Tabor's building had threatened and taunted the policemen making their initial visit. But, with a stroke of her pen, Jennifer had transformed them into the human equivalent of baby seals that had been heartlessly clubbed by police Neanderthals. The previously brash Fuerza was quoted as recounting that he and his fellow trespassers "were so terrified by the SWAT team that we debated whether it would be better to die in the burning building or go outside and face that bloodthirsty army waiting for us." The other trespassers, previously masked, now had names and life stories. They were a diverse group of artists, graduate students, social justice activists and others who cared greatly about society and wanted to use their creativity and idealism to build a more just and peaceful world. Many denounced the SWAT "fascists" who attacked their new Eden. There was no expression of gratitude for the firemen and SWAT team members who entered the burning building to look for Daniel and there was no concern expressed for the SWAT team member whose attempt to save Daniel left him seriously injured. Jennifer briefly mentioned that "a SWAT team member was injured and hospitalized" toward the end of the article without additional comment.

One key digression in the article focused on the older woman who was arrested for interfering with the SWAT team as they approached the occupied building. Readers learned that she was Kathleen Harrington-Smith, the Erwin T. Pennington Distinguished Professor of English Literature at the University. The article focused on her academic career as well as her status as an accomplished poet and long time advocate for social justice. It mentioned that Harrington-Smith had won a Pulitzer Prize for Poetry three decades earlier and that she had three grandchildren. There was very little information provided about the reasons for her arrest or how her actions created a potentially dangerous situation for the SWAT team. The message was clear. Who she was outweighed anything she might have done during the SWAT action. The MSPD had not only arrested a saintly grandmother, but also had the audacity to put one of the community's most treasured and important intellectuals in handcuffs.

Jennifer saved her best work for Daniel. She had been able to obtain a photo that made Daniel appear to be about fourteen or fifteen years old and included it in the article. Descriptions of Daniel and quotes from occupiers strongly emphasized his youth, innocence, and idealism. Others spoke at length about his career goal of becoming an attorney. His role, according to the article, had been to serve as the sentry on the top of the Tabor's building. There was no mention of the rocks he directed, or possibly threw, at the SWAT team from the roof.

Fred complemented Jennifer's work with a scathing editorial on the Morgan Springs Police Department. First, he ripped the SWAT team for turning Morgan Springs into "a veritable Fallujah, Iraq" and exposing citizens to the "extreme danger of military grade weapons that did not belong in Morgan Springs." He also compared the MSPD to the infamous Birmingham, Alabama police of the early 60s who had attacked civil rights demonstrators with water cannon and vicious dogs.

In addition to expressing anger about the "extreme danger" posed to the public, Hutchinson also complained that, by clearing the street, the police had violated the First Amendment rights of a free press since the News could not get reporters close to the action. Apparently, Hutchinson was willing to expose his staff to the "extreme danger of military grade weapons" so that his paper could fulfill its duty to get all the news to its readers.

XVI

The sun had set and, despite the fact that the air was quickly getting colder, things were heating up at Freedom Plaza. The crowd that had gathered for the six o'clock general assembly was much larger than usual. But, the general assembly meeting would be brief. The main event would be the big march to Town Hall, less than a mile away, for the Morgan Springs Town Council meeting.

The official uniform of the march was a memorial tee shirt for the martyred Daniel. The red shirt featured a monochrome of his face and read:

Daniel J. Russo
1993-2011
A Soldier for Justice

Some wore their memorial Daniel tee shirts over other shirts or thermal underwear so the shirts could be proudly displayed despite the cold weather. Others left their coats open to show off their tee shirts. Still others planned to take off their coats and show their solidarity once they got inside Town Hall. Regardless, the Mayor and Aldermen would see a sea of blood-red Daniels when they looked into the crowd at the auditorium.

The marchers began to line up. They were led by the trespassers arrested the previous Sunday who were now calling themselves the "Tabor's 13+1." The thirteen were those who were arrested at the

Tabor's building and Daniel (or at least his spirit). The "plus one" was Kathleen Harrington-Smith, who was now widely celebrated as "The Flower Lady of Morgan Springs." Like many of the marchers, she wore the red shirt with Daniel's image. To accessorize, she fashioned a necklace out of the plastic handcuffs that were used on her when she tried to interfere with the SWAT team. The other 12 arrested trespassers wore similarly fashioned necklaces to signify their status as "prisoners of conscience" and "survivors" of the tragic event.

Reverend Jimmy, as the self-appointed spiritual advisor of OMS, had hoped to be asked to march near the front of the line. However, he could understand why that honor would go to the "Flower Lady" and the other arrestees. They had put themselves on the line and suffered so they deserved the spotlight. Nonetheless, Jimmy showed up for the march in his flowing pastor's robe which allowed him to stand out among the hundreds of marchers.

Michael determined it was time to kick off the march.

"We'll be silent in Daniel's honor as we march to Town Hall," he shouted into a megaphone. "But we will all become one voice – his voice – once we get there."

In order to enhance the dramatic effect of the silent march, each participant had a candle mounted in a clear plastic cup.

The line with over 500 lit candles began to move silently in the direction of Town Hall. There had been talk of notifying the MSPD of the march so they could handle traffic. But, Michael and Katie had decided they did not want either to appear to have need of the police or to acknowledge their authority, especially since they would be castigating them at the Town Council meeting. To ensure that the march could take place without police interference, the co-leaders directed the marchers to walk single file, to stay on the sidewalks, and to obey the signals at crosswalks.

The glowing snake moved silently and gently through town. It bore no resemblance to the occupier snake that marched on the AmeriBank branch just a few weeks earlier. When the line was cut by traffic at an intersection, the marchers who crossed before the light changed would simply wait for the rest to catch up when the light changed again.

The front of the long, illuminated snake began to arrive at Town Hall about 20 minutes after leaving Freedom Plaza. The marchers extinguished their candles and started to fill up the seats in the town council chamber. Some signed up to speak at the meeting and sat near a lectern set up for citizens making comments. The meeting rules allowed people up to three minutes each to speak during the comment period of the meeting. Over 30 people signed up so, at the very least, they would be taking almost two hours of meeting time. The aldermen and the Mayor did not relish the idea of sitting through hours of citizen speeches, which were often rambling and repetitious, but they acknowledged it was essential to the democratic process.

From the dais, the Mayor watched the marchers file into the auditorium and he quickly realized that the venue's 320 seats would be filled. While some could stand in the aisles and in the back, the Fire Marshall had set the occupancy limit at 375 people. Many would have to watch by closed circuit TV in the lobby or other parts of the Town Hall. The Mayor busied himself pretending to look at memos and in pre-meeting conversations with aldermen to avoid the angry glares of the assembling audience. At seven o'clock, he banged his gavel and called the meeting to order.

"This meeting will now come to order," he intoned grimly.

What was left of the quiet dignity of the candlelight march dissolved instantly at the mere sound of the Mayor's voice.

A voice shouted "Blood on your hands." Like an echo, "Blood on your hands" came from another part of the auditorium. And then from a third. By the fourth iteration, the entire red-shirted crowd was chanting in unison, "Blood on your hands. Blood on your hands."

Worthington looked across the auditorium and, except for the absence of pitchforks and torches, the Mayor thought he was viewing a scene from a classic Frankenstein movie where the angry villagers appear at the gate of the castle to kill the monster. He did not look very mayoral in this setting and, in addition to the hundreds at the Town Hall, many other Morgan Springs residents would be watching the meeting on the community access channel. Steven realized that, in addition to running this meeting, he probably had only minutes to salvage his political career.

He banged his gavel again and shouted into the microphone, "You need to remain orderly so we can conduct this meeting. I know a lot of you want to speak and we will give you that opportunity. Citizen comments are the first thing on the agenda. But, if we can't get started, we will clear the auditorium."

The noise barely subsided.

"We have a lot of business to conduct tonight. I repeat, we will clear this auditorium if necessary."

The crowd noise diminished a little more.

The Mayor gestured to two policemen and they appeared at the front of the auditorium to show that they were ready to start the process of directing people out of the auditorium.

There was still some crowd noise but Steven knew he could be heard over it without having to yell into his microphone.

"Thank you. Thank you," he said as soothingly as he could. "We're glad to have you here tonight. Like I said, the citizen comment period is our first order of business. But please, allow me to say a few words before we get underway."

The crowd was still restless, but he had their attention.

"Let me tell you a little bit about your Mayor, Steven Worthington," he began. He heard a few groans as he began to talk about himself in the third person, but he forged ahead. "Steven Worthington was marching for gay rights years ago when it wasn't popular. Steven Worthington has spent many nights outside of Eastern State Prison at vigils on the nights of executions. Steven Worthington chose to use his legal education to assist undocumented immigrant workers rather than to help corporations and banks screw the little guy. Steven Worthington has been arrested multiple times for civil disobedience. Steven Worthington has worked tirelessly to get progressive candidates elected to local, state, and federal offices."

As he spoke of his noble deeds, the crowd quieted, and the Mayor knew that his self homage was being heard. Steven could sense that the recitation of his progressive bona fides had instilled some guilt in the occupiers, and he felt the smug joy of righteous indignation. His comfort level grew and he began to luxuriate in the sound of his own words. Just a few weeks earlier, he had been almost begging the occupiers not to defecate on Washington Street. But now, he felt he was getting back in control.

He voice rose a bit to his finale. "Steven Worthington," he paused for emphasis, "has cast aside his privilege to spend his entire adult life working for peace, equality, and justice." He paused again. "And that will include justice for Daniel Russo."

The audience now belonged to the Mayor and he enjoyed his brief respite. But, they had all come to Town Hall to express anger and demand action. Steven was no longer the target, but their anger and energy remained. Steven would now start the process of redirecting that anger and energy.

Of course, the Mayor had no intention of blaming the MSPD himself. The people who would speak would take care of that for him, especially since he had seeded the speaker list with some of his supporters. He was fairly sure of the types of comments the occupiers would make. In his estimation, an overwhelming majority of the thirty people who had signed up to speak would practically beg him to do what he had already planned – to authorize a citizen committee to review the incident and the actions of the Police Department. He knew most of the people who would be on the committee as well as the one alderman who would be the committee's Town Council representative. He also knew that most of the members harbored a reflexive disdain for law enforcement. The results of any review were practically a foregone conclusion.

The parliamentarian began calling the names of the speakers who wanted their three minutes to talk.

The Town Council settled in for what would be over 90 minutes of speeches. Some of the speakers were articulate, delivered carefully prepared remarks, and respected the three minute time limit. However, many more used their turns at the microphone to rant angrily, as if more volume and invective would strengthen the points which had already been made. Regardless of the tone or coherence of the comments, it appeared that most speakers were laying responsibility for the incident at the Tabor's building at the feet of the Morgan Springs Police Department.

The parliamentarian called out the twenty-sixth name on the list. "Burke Thornton."

Burke walked to the podium. Because he was wearing Dockers and a button down shirt and was certainly middle-aged, the members of the audience correctly guessed that he was not part of the group that marched to Town Hall. Burke put on his reading glasses and pulled out a sheet of paper with his prepared remarks.

Looking in the direction of the Mayor and Aldermen, he began, "Thank you for this opportunity to speak. I know it has been a difficult week and a long night already." He took a breath and continued.

"A young man is dead, a member of our police force has suffered an injury that may end his career, a downtown building has been destroyed, and our town's reputation has been seriously damaged. Naturally, we want to know why this happened and who is responsible.

"I have heard all sorts of reasons, but it seems that most want to blame the Morgan Springs Police Department.

"However, I would suggest that it was our community itself that played the greatest role in this tragedy. From its first day several weeks ago, this so-called occupation has been nothing but a series of provocations and attacks on our community. And each of these provocations was ignored. First, Freedom Plaza, a public space for the use and enjoyment of everyone in this community, was taken over by a handful of people who prevented anyone else from using it. Almost no one said anything. Second, these occupiers claimed to speak for all of us, or almost all of us, with the exception of some hated, One Percent minority enemy. We talk endlessly about our diverse community, yet remained silent while self-appointed spokesmen claimed to be the voice of everyone. Third, the occupiers provided literature that celebrated anarchy, destruction, and murder. Again, silence. Or, we attributed it to their youthful zeal and naiveté while ignoring its truly disturbing nature. Fourth, when the occupiers engaged in criminal acts – the vandalism of businesses on Washington Street and an attack on a child at St. Paul's – we pretended that the responsible individuals were outliers who had nothing to do with what was going on in Freedom Plaza. Finally, the occupiers decided to take over private property and ultimately destroyed it. Judging by what I have heard tonight, many of us are still in denial about the nature of Occupy Morgan Springs.

"The regrettable truth is that our society was attacked and we failed, refused actually, to defend it – again and again and again. We failed to defend Morgan Springs against those who had no regard for this community, its people, it traditions, the democratic process, or property rights. Their behavior was beneath that of animals, and yet we adopted them as community mascots. We shouldn't be surprised that, in only a few weeks, the occupation of Freedom Plaza, which we cheered and celebrated, escalated to the senseless tragedy at the old Tabor's building.

"We love to think that our community is so enlightened and that our so-called progressivism has moved us forward. But history has shown repeatedly that when some group decides that it uniquely represents society, that only it can speak for "the people," and that the only thing that stands in the way of progress and happiness is some tiny and evil minority, it never ends well. Not in 1917. Not in 1933. Not in Morgan Springs.

"I don't know why we invited this insanity into our community with open arms. Perhaps we wanted the vicarious thrill of storming some Bastille. It could be that we were bored and the novelty of this occupation added some excitement to our comfortable, but predictable lives. Maybe an occupation was just what all the cool people in all the other cool communities are doing and we didn't want to feel like Morgan Springs wasn't in the club.

"This community isn't perfect and never will be. But we have been enthusiastically supporting a movement to replace what we have – a basically sound society and civilization – with what? An assault on a bank? Taking over and destroying private property? Recreating the Neolithic era in Freedom Plaza? This is not a plan for the future. This is not progress. This is anarchy and nihilism.

"Our community owes its affluence and good fortune to our larger American society and its values. In fact, Morgan Springs benefits far more than other people in our state or in most of the rest of the nation. Yet, our response to Occupy Morgan Springs demonstrates an eagerness to throw these things away.

"Once we succeed in destroying what we have, we will be the ones who miss it the most."

Burke returned to his seat immediately after speaking and was not the least bit concerned that he made the occupants of the adjacent seats uncomfortable. Those around him looked straight ahead stiffly as if they were afraid that their body language or head movements might suggest they knew Thornton, or even worse, had come to the meeting with him. Some occupiers used the safety of their distance to stare at him. Burke could almost feel their hateful eyes and, if he actually saw a pair looking in his direction, would lock onto the face that held them until the angry face turned elsewhere.

XVII

Like everyone in Morgan Springs, Linda knew that the Town Council meeting would be filled with fireworks so she eagerly watched from home on the public access channel that carried local meetings. The chamber had several fixed cameras which captured the dais, the entire chamber, and the lectern where people spoke. Whoever was operating the cameras did a good job of capturing the restlessness and murmurings in the chamber after Burke's speech. It was clear that his three minutes had inflamed the audience.

Linda believed that what Burke said made a lot of sense.

Opinions about Burke Thornton's comments were being formulated and immediately disseminated. Texts, tweets, and postings began flying back and forth in the chamber as well as throughout the community. His name was on the lips – or fingers – of all who were engrossed in Morgan Springs politics. He was now the lightning rod in an increasingly violent political storm.

Linda began to peruse her Facebook "news" on her phone. She immediately saw a post from the recently rehabilitated Julia Mendaris. Like Linda and many others in Morgan Springs, Julia had been watching the town council meeting and weighed in on Thornton's three minutes in front of the microphone. "This guy is a plumber. I don't think he even went to college. What was he talking about? Idiots like him should know better than to waste the Town Council's time."

Thornton was not faring well in the court of public opinion among Julia's 874 Facebook "friends." Seventeen people had already commented and 22 "liked" Julia's attack on Thornton by the time Linda saw the post (a mere 15 minutes after Thornton's transgressive speech). The wave of online applause in the form of supportive comments and "likes" showed that Julia's redemption was complete and she had been readmitted to the fold of Morgan Springs' *bien-pensants*.

Linda was so engrossed in Julia's post and the growing list of comments that she almost overlooked a recent post from her older son, Justin. She had not heard from him in over a week. Justin reported excitedly to the Facebook community that he had become the co-leader of an Occupy Wall Street offshoot and that his group had occupied a city park near his campus. The post included a photo of Justin and another man standing by a tent. Other tents in the photo background showed that this occupier camp was very similar to the one in Freedom Plaza.

Linda's mind quickly went to dark places. She thought about Daniel Russo, almost the same age as Justin, and his senseless death. She wondered if circumstances had been different, how many more young people might have been killed in the fire. She had also been following Occupy Wall Street activity in other parts of the country. The *New York Times* reported rapes at the Occupy Wall Street encampment at Zucotti Park in Manhattan. She saw video of an occupier mob going on a rampage in Oakland. Across the country, there were reports of vandalism, arson, assaults, deaths, and even murders.

Much had changed in Morgan Springs since that first Monday morning in October when Occupy Morgan Springs suddenly appeared in Freedom Plaza. Linda's excitement during those heady first hours in Morgan Springs had given way to profound concern about what might happen to her own son in his occupier experience.

Linda returned to the orgy of Burke Thornton bashing that Julia had started. In the past few minutes, the thread had moved from a discussion of why Thornton was a terrible human being to ideas of how to punish him for his unpardonable affront to community sensibilities.

"This guy has a big plumbing services company," one wrote. "We should organize a boycott to hit this guy where it will hurt him the most . . . his wallet. Clearly, he cares more about making money than about justice or this community."

Others joined in with promises of calling anyone but Thornton's company for their future plumbing issues while delighting in the prospect of bringing financial harm to this uppity plumber who got out of line.

Linda knew this was mostly idle chatter. She recalled a Thanksgiving holiday several years before when her brother-in-law's family stayed in her home and another family joined them for Thanksgiving dinner. The water heater died and Thornton's company was the only one who could send someone on short notice. One of Thornton's plumbers, missing part of his Thanksgiving with his own family, salvaged the holiday weekend for Linda and her guests.

She knew she would call Thornton Plumbing in the future if she needed those services. She guessed that many of those boldly talking about a boycott would do the same, just like many of them talked about how much they hated Wal-Mart yet would sneak in from time to time when they really needed to buy something quickly and cheaply.

Like him or not, Burke Thornton was just one of those people who kept civilization together.

Linda thought the posturing she saw unfolding on Julia's Facebook page was ridiculous. Only three weeks ago, Julia was a pariah for saying exactly what she thought. Now, she was receiving approbation because she skewered Burke Thornton for saying things Julia might possibly agree with herself. But, Linda was also envious of Julia. Morgan Springs was the type of place that could give its residents great confidence that they were especially enlightened. And, because they saw this enlightenment as exceptional, they took great pleasure in knowing they were in exclusive company. Linda wanted to feel the confidence and pleasure that Julia was feeling.

Linda returned to Justin's post and looked at his photo again. She had last seen him just before he returned to college, but he looked very different now. In this picture, he looked taller, more mature, and more serious than he had looked just three months earlier. He was a leader who exuded charisma. He looked like someone who would capture the imagination of Morgan Springs.

She swelled with pride and hit the "share" button so all her peers would know what her son was doing and she could be the very first to show public support for Justin's exciting new venture.